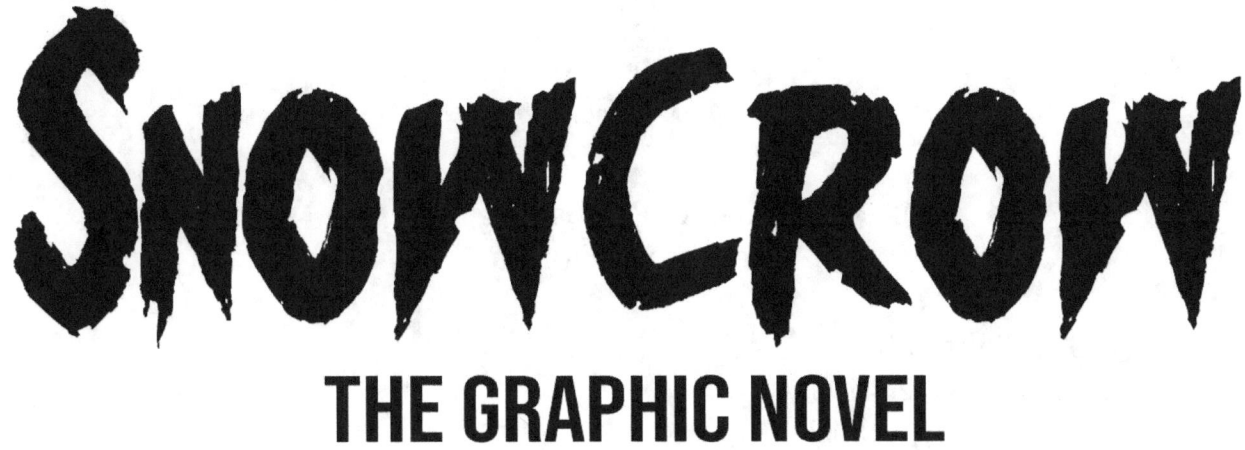

SNOWCROW

THE GRAPHIC NOVEL

BLAKE ALB

ILLUSTRATIONS BY

JOHN DAVIES

World Castle Publishing, LLC
Pensacola, Florida

Copyright © 2025 Blake Alb
Hardcover ISBN: 9798891264793
Paperback ISBN: 9798891264809
eBook ISBN: 9798891264816
First Edition World Castle Publishing, LLC, October 6, 2025
http://www.worldcastlepublishing.com

Licensing Notes

Blake Alb: Story, dialogue, and panel descriptions
John Davies: Illustrations
Lieh Pena: Lettering
Edited by Karen Fuller
Test readers: Denise, Shannon, and Terrence

Foreword by Hermione Lee, author of the Otherworld Trilogy.

Every book is unique because no two authors are the same. But if the witty, humorous, yet thought-provoking Snowcrow was written by another author, would it have the same effect? There is something irreplaceable and unprecedented about Blake Alb's writing style. Few—if any—writers can imitate his original, creative wordplay and ingenious plot.

In Snowcrow, readers follow the daily life of Teddy Jales, a far-from-average boy who always entertains bigger-than-life notions. Alb does not let Teddy's age constrict and confine him. Although Teddy is only fourteen, he has an old soul and is no doubt wiser than the adults around him. However, even intelligent youths must grow, and Teddy is plagued by a myriad of doubts when a series of unexplainables transpire. In the end, Teddy grows mentally and emotionally, grasping the importance to "seize the day" and "enjoy the present," a message today's fast-paced society should hear and take to heart.

Snowcrow shattered my stereotypes about books and altered the traditional definition of "fine" prose. It would not be an exaggeration to say it changed my life and perception of writing as well. And, very different from the preachy, indoctrinated coming-of-age tales, this one was written in a new, original, fresh, and creative voice. Sprinkled throughout the pages, the wordplay, puns, similes, anagrams, idioms, alliteration, and anthropomorphism always makes me chuckle. The metaphors of life and the strange, thrilling incidents will keep readers flipping the pages, desperate to learn the ending.

Without gore, graphic violence, or bloody murders, the essence of Snowcrow lies in the inexplicable coincidences and illogical occurrences. Alb portrays the setting, the ambiance, and the scenes in such meticulous detail that readers find themselves effortlessly whisked into the book. Teddy, raw and believable, has a quirkiness that brings a smile to my lips. However, like everyone else, he has his flaws to overcome—apophenia, for one—but his charming characteristics and endearing personality are enough to keep readers hooked. An unconventional hero who thinks outside the box and refuses to drift into conformity, he is an exceptional protagonist in the field of literature.

Snowcrow is a perfect combination of humor, wordplay, literary techniques, and a gripping plot. It is a veritable trail mix of successful qualities one can expect from a masterpiece of a novella. There may come a day when Snowcrow is seen as a timeless classic—not only for adults or young adults, but to every person in the world—regardless of age, gender, race, or nationality.

Preface

Astute readers will notice some slight differences between the Snowcrow novella and the graphic novel. These kinds of discrepancies in works of fiction can understandably raise questions (or provoke the ire) in fans regarding the accuracy, time-line, canon, or "historical record" of the original universe (calling the author's world-building into question). There are various ways in which authors have "made peace" with deviations in logical events or continuity (sometimes years after a work has ended).

But should there be a statute of limitations on canon or retroactive continuity (i.e. retcon)? Can the author of a 10 volume book or manga "suddenly decide" that the entire story was a dream? Can an author "suddenly decide" that a previous work is no longer canon, like the annulment of a marriage? Authors do not have a Code of Ethics that I am aware of. But if they did, perhaps a statute of limitations on canon or retconning isn't such a bad idea. Some might say that changing events, even in a fictitious world, can be just as egregious as an anachronism in a work of non-fiction or historical drama. Certainly there are times when retconning can make us feel cheated, especially when events are drastically re-explained or changed altogether (really putting the "con" in retcon).

Some authors will side-step the issue by saying something is "no longer canon." Hopefully at the very least the author will "give you permission" to treat it like a "side story." While this may appease many readers, it might still run the risk of leaving die-hard fans of the original work feeling disgruntled or cheated, as the original version may have been their preferred version of events in the "official timeline."

So the question remains. How do I rationalize any slight changes in Snowcrow between the novella and graphic novel versions? I can't help but feel hopeful that there is indeed a manner that can leave all parties feeling satisfied. As such, readers can treat each version as if an "alternate reality" or "alternate world line" in the same universe. In this way, both realities can be considered canon. That way, neither one of the books need be minimized or considered a "side story." So whichever events the reader prefers, that can be their favored alternate reality! Thanks for listening to (or rather seeing) my little (scant) rant.

CHAPTER 01:

WHEN HELL....

....FREEZES OVER

January 28, 2016 (Thursday)

Dear Diary,

There are many kinds of journaling. There is the "free association" variety, where you proliferate words all over the page like a Cobb word salad, as if it's some sort of Freudian gateway to the recesses of one's unconscious. Journaling can also include poetry, song lyrics, and short stories. And who's to say sketching can't be considered journaling? Is not a sketch also a form of communication, not unlike the hieroglyphics of old? One could even go about creating their own Rorschach ink blots and deciphering them. But what about the ol' standby "Dear Diary?" I suppose it has an element of free association to it (David Hinckley once said my diary was the stuff of entitled and self-centered drama queens). By any stretch, I like to think of it as a historical record, an artifact that a rabble of aliens might find in a rock pile a thousand years from now. Let's just hope they find it more interesting than stick figures on a cave wall.

But what is the point of history, anyway? Human civilization never seems to learn from its mistakes. Battles are fought, wars are "won." But how much of it boils down to the petty clashing of egos? Talk about "petty officers!" This is especially true when each side doubles down, and spit balls evolve into wedgies, and wedgies evolve into swirlies, and swirlies evolve into rocket launchers (I think that's how the Arms Race got started). My Animal Psychology professor Mrs. Robbins once said that behind the veneer of "noble causes" all wars are, at their core, a form of population control as humans battle it out for scarce resources (as if rams butting heads atop a mountain peak). "Humans are animals by the end of the day," she manages to squeeze into every lecture. She added that the clashing of different colored flags is just a smokescreen to hide the fact that both sides lost the battle and the war before it even started. Talk about flags being cut from the same cloth. King of the Hill may be rough and tumble, but it was never meant to be about population control (more like popularity control). Either way, I don't think that's the hill David wanted to die on.

Speaking of that classy classroom lady Mrs. Robbins, just today she taught us about a macaque supermom that raised triplets in the wild. She sounded more like a mother reading a bedtime story (she even had the sweeping arm motions and body language to boot). All she needed was the flashlight. And just like an Aesop's Fable, she didn't hesitate to turn the academic lesson into a moral lesson about how the students wouldn't be so tired in class if we went to bed earlier. I guess she mistook a classroom lecture for the kind of lecture that parents give their kids when they sneak home after dark (at least she didn't put her hands on her hips). And to think Mrs. Robbins didn't have any kids of her own, singular, plural, or otherwise! Maybe she has a macaque monkey.

Thursday came and went, and so did David Hinckley. Despite "dead" being just about the easiest word in the English language to pronounce, David was pronounced dead on arrival just as he got to the hospital. Yeah, I know. I can just hear Jane saying "too soon" after that last sentence. Can't she just humor my attempt at humor? David and I may not have been as thick as thieves, but I would never wish ill-will towards him.

Amongst the land of the living, Jeremy Pegg was the most affected. He spent a good part of the afternoon in the counselor's office (and not because of his crush on Sylvia). According to the rumor mill, he could be on suicide watch for a couple of weeks. I can still hear Jeremy's voice in my head as the ambulance drove away, shouting through his tears: "Take me instead! I want to be the one to die!! Let David live!" I hope Sylvia can convince Jeremy that in life accidents do happen, even when playing King of the Hill. You know what they say, t's always fun until someone falls off a hill of snow and hits a fire hydrant... David wasn't even king for a day before he learned that it was lonely at the top. I guess it's not always good to be king.

The ambulance may as well have been a hearse as it hauled David away. And why was his cell phone inside the snowman? Was there something supernatural about that snowman? Jane didn't seem too concerned about my "conspiracy theory." She thought the phone must have just gotten there by accident when David took a jab at the snowman's abdomen. And why was the snowman facing the red fire hydrant? I could have sworn he was looking straight ahead before (like any snowman ever). Jane seems to think that when David punched the snowman the coal in his eyes and mouth must have fell out and some kid slapped them back in his head sideways. At any rate, the entire event was unsettling to say the least. As for David Hinckley? Let's just hope he found reprieve and repose in death. Needless to say, today a chill went down my spine, and it wasn't from the winter air.

CHAPTER 2:

"ICY SCRUTINY" AND "LEISURE SEIZURES"

ABOUT SIX WEEKS AGO, DECEMBER 14, 2015 (MONDAY).

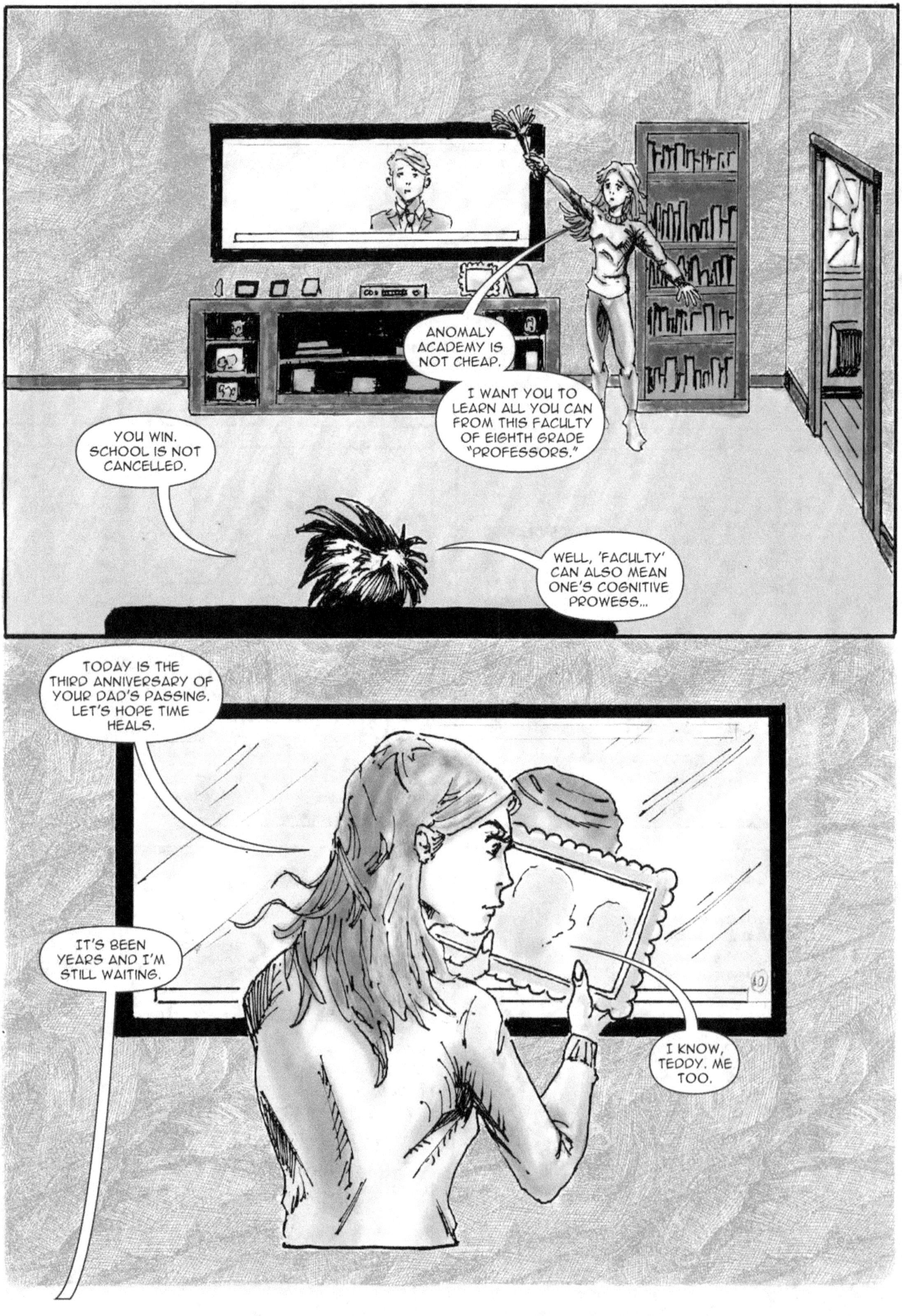

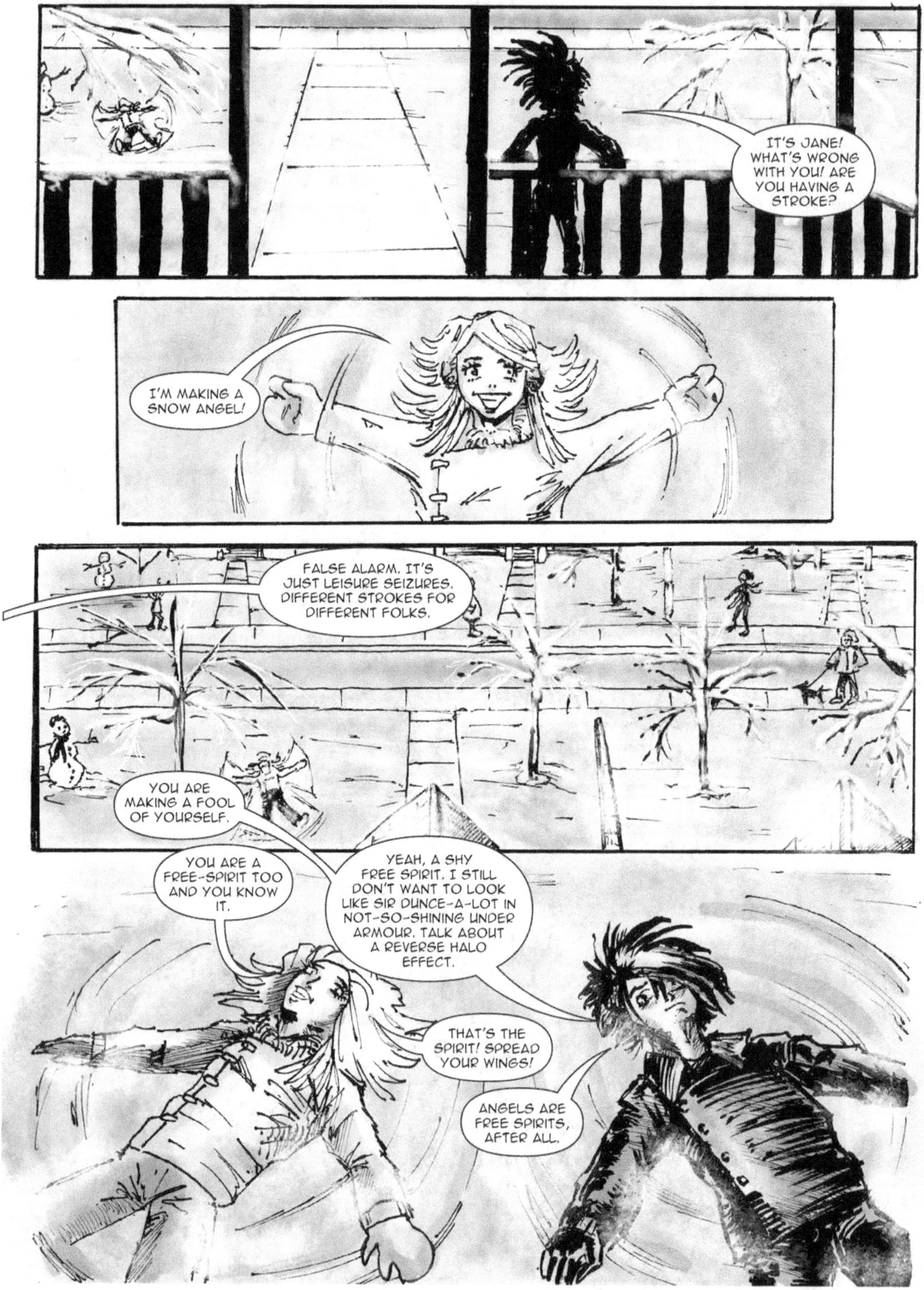

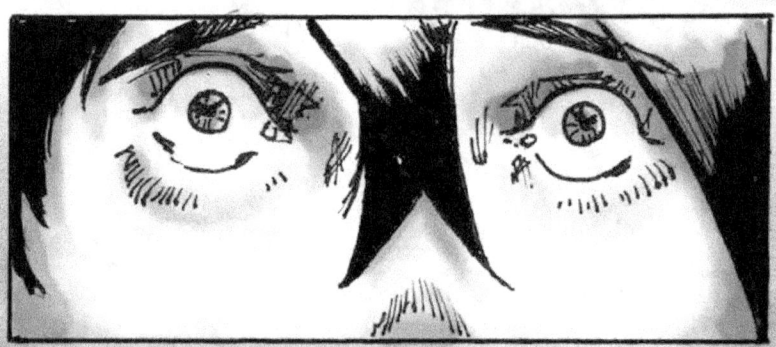

December 14, 2015 (Monday)

Dear Diary,

Sure enough we had school today, despite our mini-blizzard (it was more like the small size at a Dairy Queen). If anything, it just made the day worse, as I slipped on the ice coming off the bus. And being Monday and all, that also meant I had my appointment with Sylvia Koch, the school counselor.

And just so you know, Mr. Diary, the decision to see her wasn't from my own volition. It was at the behest of none other than Karen Tales, my mother-in-chief. She thinks I need to process the recent losses in my life, such as the death of my grandmother and dad. I'm still not sure how revisiting old wounds can be therapeutic. My hunch is that mom has a hidden agenda to keep me sane enough to keep getting good grades (given the expense of Anomaly Academy).

Today Sylvia addressed "intrinsic motivation" and "extrinsic motivation." She said if I come to see her only because my mother is making me that would constitute extrinsic motivation. But if I get to the point where I want to see her, then it would be intrinsic motivation. She said this is the preferable of the two as I would have "want and need alignment" where you "want what you need." She said if you can reach that pinnacle it's smoother sailing from there. It sure doesn't sound like Nirvana to me. More like a glutton for punishment.

Sylvia also taught Developmental Psychology. Today we talked about Eric Erickson's 8 Stages of Conflict. I'm not gonna lie, it freaked me out a bit, especially the final stage "Integrity vs. Despair." Was this like the ultimate three-form boss battle? The final stage after passing through 7 other lesser battles? Is "Integrity" the way to the "good ending" and "Despair" the pathway to the "bad ending?" The whole affair reminded me of games like Hudson's Adventure Island on the classic NES. Its not just the damage from foes that reduces your health, but also the passing of time itself. For all I know, I could be dreaming right now. Or maybe I am just some random character in someone's graphic novel or manga. How can we possibly know? I find it all rather disconcerting.

Since I am in a morbid sort of mood, I find it rather creepy that there is a skeleton inside me right now. At this very moment! And to think it's animated, just like in the scary movies. You just can't see it as it's covered in blood and guts. One would think that would make things even scarier. Outta sight, outta mind I guess. Still, I can't help but feel that our skeletons are marionette puppets, and the muscles that pull the bones are the strings. But that only begs the question, if muscles move the bones, what moves the muscles? I suppose that would be the brain. But what "strings" pull the brain? I suppose that would be our genetic makeup and DNA. Humans really are just organic computers, with blood, bones, and guts instead of cogs, wheels, grease, and oil. Where is the "puppet master" in all of this? My grandpa Clint always talked about how people make "choices" and have "free will" as if it was all about mind over matter. But why do we make the choices we make? Can a "choice" really be considered a causal factor? I brought this up to Sylvia. She said that people do make choices, this is true, but these choices are "determined" by the forces of nature and nurture (making a "choice" an effect rather than a cause).

I brought up the topic of determinism to David one time, and he just said I think too much and I needed a girlfriend. He added to this sage wisdom and stated that I need to get more muscles if I ever hoped to go past the friend zone with Jane. I didn't have the heart to tell him that being "friend zoned" was a step up from my usual being "acquaintance zoned" (and unfriended as soon as I wore out my welcome). I was a bit of a chick-magnet alright, the kind that repels instead of attracts.

I didn't have much time to craft the perfect comeback so I went for the low-hanging fruit: "I don't see you with anybody." And to that all he said was "there are plenty of fish in the sea." My lips flapped before my filter had a chance to turn on: "I hope they like bullheads or bottom feeders."

If it weren't for Professor Humis walking down the hall at that precise moment David may have tried to tune me up a bit, if only to maintain his lofty position in the pecking order and keep the locker room as his turf. I guess threats and aggression were his way of marking his territory. At least he didn't pee on my locker like a dog marking a fire hydrant. 'Tis a shame social media doesn't have "enemy requests." I would be sure to send him one.

Maybe David was right and I spent too much time in my head. Maybe that's what Jane meant when she called me "Ted the Head." Let's just hope that title makes me sound more famous rather than infamous. At this point it could go either way. I just wish David wouldn't rent so much space in my head. Or maybe I just didn't suffer idiotic, reprobate, moronic, and jug-headed fools gladly. Don't get me wrong. It's not as if I am the life of the party either. If anything, I'm more like the "death of the party," the search party kind that looks for a homicide victim.

Soon it will be 2016, an election year. If only the rules of debate applied to politics. Who decides who won the debate? Each side just declares their favored orator as the winner. If only a debate referee would pin down the loser on the mat, count to 10, and raise the hand of the victor in sweet victory. If only truth could be measured with a thermometer. I think I will just buy a roll of "I voted" stickers, pretend I voted, and call it a day.

Speaking of Jane, she asked me today about snowmen and snow angels and it donned on me that snowmen resemble scarecrows. After all, they can both be ragged and disconcerting with their sticks and stones. And we all know from the song what "sticks and stones" can do. But if scarecrows are meant to scare crows away from eating crops, what are these "snowcrows" meant to scare?

CHAPTER 3:
WHERE THERE IS SMOKE THERE ARE MIRRORS

DECEMBER 18, 2015 (FRIDAY).

"ACCORDING TO 'THE HIDDEN MESSAGES IN WATER' BY MASARU EMOTO..."

...WATER CAN TAKE ON A NEGATIVE OR POSITIVE VALENCE DEPENDING ON THE TOXICITY...

...OF THE EMOTIONAL ENERGY LINGERING IN ITS PROXIMITY.

SOMEHOW I DON'T THINK THAT QUESTION HAS EVER BEEN UTTERED BEFORE.

HEY, PROFESSOR HUMIS, ARE YOU SAYING THAT SENTIENT WATER PREFERS CLASSICAL MUSIC OVER HEAVY-METAL?

IT'S NICE TO SEE SOME YULETIDE CLASS PARTICIPATION FROM OUR MR. HINCKLEY. DAVID SHOULD CONSIDER ADDING A FEW BELLS TO HIS LEATHER JACKET.

DAVID COMING TO CLASS WITH BELLS ON?

TIS THE SEASON.

DAVID HAS A POINT. IF BEAUTY IS IN THE EYE OF THE BEHOLDER, WHO'S TO SAY WHAT MUSIC IS TOXIC? NOT THAT I BELIEVE ANY OF THIS ANYWAY.

PERHAPS THESE WATER LUMINARIES NEED TO TAKE A LESSON FROM FOOTLOOSE.

EVERY MORNING FOR THE LAST THREE WEEKS, I HAVE BEEN SENDING NEGATIVE VIBES TO THE JAR ON STAGE LEFT.

I HAVE ALSO BEEN HARNESSING MY POSITIVE ENERGY AND SAYING NICETIES AND SWEET NOTHINGS TO THE RICE IN THE OTHER JAR.

AT LEAST WE DON'T HAVE TO BRING RICE TO THE WEDDING!

WELL, DAVID, I WOULDN'T SAY THAT. BUT YOU COULD SAY THE RICE AND I ARE AT LEAST ON SPEAKING TERMS.

IN THE INTERESTS OF SCIENCE, I THINK WE SHOULD CALL ONE "VICE RICE" AND THE OTHER "NICE RICE."

SHEESH, THE PROFESSOR IS NOW TALKING TO RICE.

TALK ABOUT GOING AGAINST THE GRAIN.

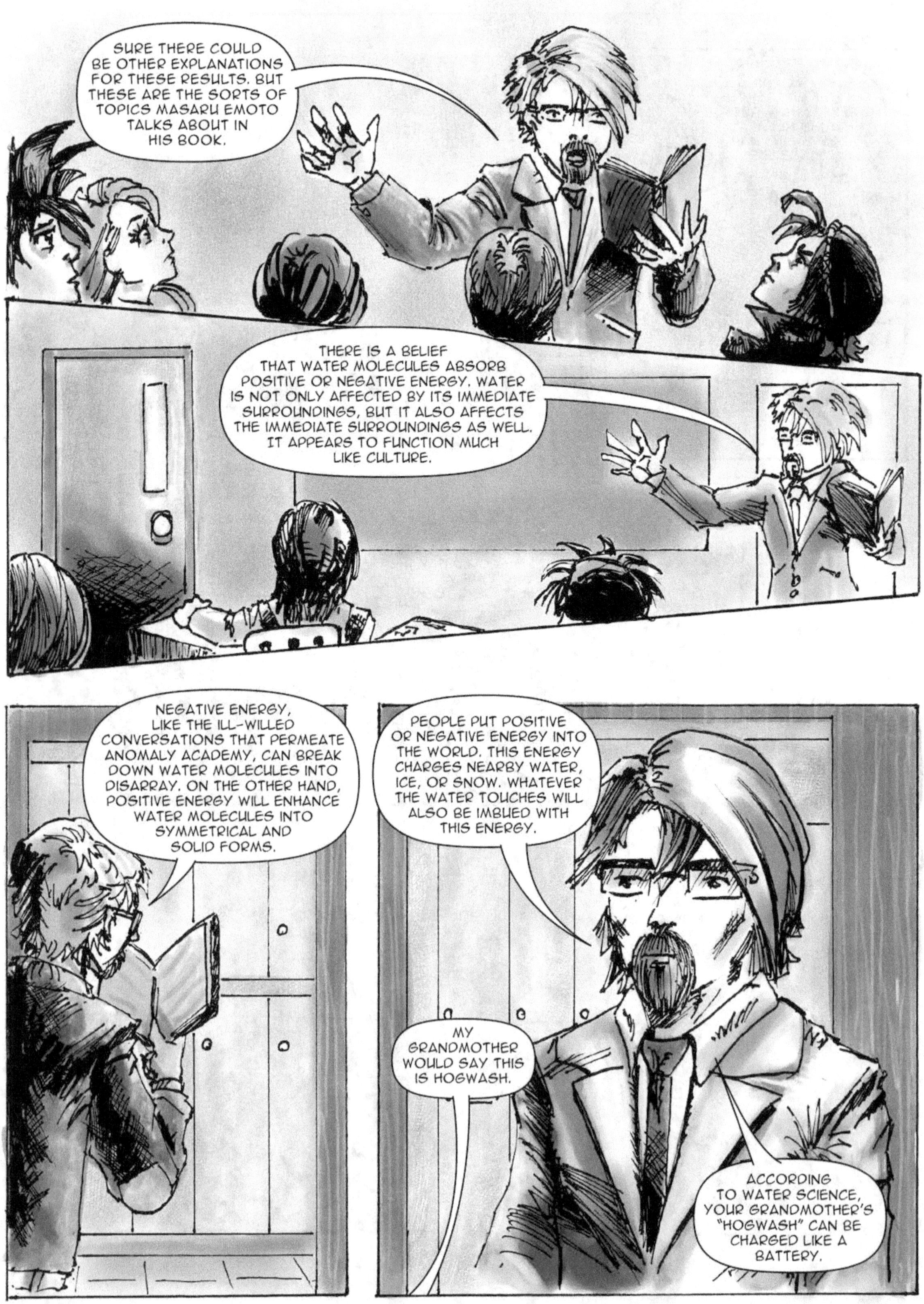

December 18, 2015

Dear Diary,

Professor Humis was talking about how Work equals Force-times-Distance today. He also added a second equation (hours worked X hourly wage). He used David as a shining pinnacle of someone who could benefit from either equation.

Talk about double Jeopardy (which it appears David watches). Then again, in math two negatives do make a positive. So maybe two wrongs do make a right (and David may be onto something with his laissez-faire lifestyle).

This morning David was nominated vice president of the Student Council. But that was before he was caught smoking a cigar and drinking Jägermeister in the restroom trying his best to do both at the same time (he said it was for the interests of science). Humis also heard him swearing at the janitor for not cleaning the vomit stain in front of the English room. So what was David's defense? He insisted that when he said "damn" he was talking about the beaver kind. Who knew David (or the janitor for that matter) were into ethology?

Needless to say, David was forced to resign his post as vice president by the afternoon. I guess he must have thought being vice president meant having more vices than anyone else in the class. The whole debacle makes me want to have a New Year's resolution to be more lazy. Maybe I will sleep nine hours a day instead of eight. I can call it a sleep study and do it "for the interests of science."

David Hinckley sure is a piece of work, and I don't mean 'The Starry Night' by Vincent Van Gogh. He arrived to Anomaly Academy less than a month ago. So after getting to know him for a month, what can I say about him? There's a mighty fine line between a class-act and an ass-hat. He's a regular of the back-row nosebleed section and Peanut Gallery. Still, I gotta give him some mad props for showing up, even if he was the kind of guy who would need to add "Potty Trained" to his resume to fill up the page (and still maintain a twelve point font). But at least he was present. Still, if he skipped school more often he could stay under the radar more. Either way, he wore his indiscretions like a badge of honor. But to the rest of the English speaking world, his sordid name was generally held in disrepute—other than the comic relief he provided. After all, we are talking about the guy that thinks a "coat check" is when a career counselor inspects and approves your jacket for a job interview. And the only thing a "white paper" meant for him was unfinished homework. This was the same guy that thought the "Battle of the Bulge" was when two men compared sizes of certain appendages (our David had an uncanny ability to turn anything into an innuendo or double entendre). "It's a gift," he says. But what do you expect from a guy who has a cockroach as a spirit animal?

What I found most odd was how such an irascible underachiever was even sent to our "one of a kind diamond in the rough" school that was christened Anomaly Academy in the first place. And then Jane explained all the nepotism involved. His grandfather founded the place! But any way you diced it, David Hinckley was an anomaly among outliers.

So who was I when compared to David? I wouldn't say I was an angel or teacher's pet. Nor was I the archetypal recalcitrant rebel. I guess you could say that I was "sweet and salty," a madcap "freek" (spelled with two e's) or a "geak" (spelled with an e and an a). I was an eclectic trail mix of Nerds, Scottie Dogs, beef jerky, corn chips, corn nuts, and Andes mints. So while I considered myself to be that aberrant non-conformist at heart, I did have some insecurities that made it difficult for me to want to stand out like a sore thumb from a hitch-hiker's hand. And that would explain my apprehension to make snow angels with Jane the other day. Things like that just seemed to have a way of making me feel as if a tap dancer under a giant spotlight (and at any given moment I would be yanked off stage with a giant cane). I guess one could say that I was something of a class clown, at least the sad kind.

I wouldn't say my family was a faery tale (unless we are talking sad ones like Bluebeard). When dad and grandma died that was when our once-nuclear family went nuclear (complete with fallout, as the neighbors on both sides of our house have quit talking to mom altogether). But despite the dysfunction of all the back and forth arguing and shouting, things at least never got physical. It would still be nice if one could "assume no family friction" like in a physics problem.

It was ironic that I was born on Labor day (an omen in more ways than one). But as to whether this was mere serendipity or the stuff of Divine Providence, the jury was not only out, but it was hung. Regardless, I hold two birthday parties every year (I am a fan of the two party system). And as for my spirit animal? That was reserved either for the walking stick or sea cucumber. Spirit plant? Venus Fly Trap. No dispute.

People assumed that I was the valedictorian type. But that was incorrect. Salutatorian? That wasn't out of the question. But there I was, sitting in class, self-effacing yet soaking it all in, like a piece of strawberry shortcake sponging up berries and cream. Not that this was my favorite food, mind. That one was reserved for trail mix, hands down (in the bowl, that is). After all, a well-blended sweet and salty trail mix is the epitome of when the whole is greater than the sum of its parts. But you gotta get the ratio just right. Just mixing random odds and ends together is not a proper trail mix. That is just being superfluous. And there is nothing super about that. At least not any more super than an outstanding warrant can be called outstanding or the Great Depression can be called great.

My mother liked to liken me as resembling that fictional mascot who went by the epithet of "Hardware Hank." I would tend to agree, at least if he was more sullen, dressed in black, had longer hair, smiled less, painted more landscapes than houses, was more neurotic, didn't wear a baseball cap, and didn't know a thing about hardware.

Professor Humis impressed me as usual today. They say that employers don't want people who are too smart, as they may not be people-persons with the charisma and decorum needed to be a team player (or sycophant). Somehow Humis must have slipped through the cracks (they must have cast a blind eye to the fact that he ate his steak with a spoon). Don't get me wrong, Humis was not a man of hubris. Today he supplemented his academic lesson with a motivational one. He shared how he used to hate homework, but used frappuccino and junk food as a self-reward to bribe himself into getting it done. He went on to pontificate about the importance of discipline, patience, and delayed gratification and how these were just as important as intelligence (and could only be obtained from the School of Hard Knocks). For all the time I spent at that school I should have a master's degree by now.

But there was another caveat that separated our good professor from your typical dyed-in-the-tweed variety. He had a certain penchant and passion for certain subjects of a more pseudoscientific or metaphysical nature (ghosts, aliens, time travel, and the like). But he drew the line at bigfoot (that was too far-fetched). Today Professor Humis talked about "sentient water," and how water could supposedly pick up negative or positive vibes from the stimuli surrounding it and become charged. His copy of the book "The Hidden Messages in Water" by Masaru Emoto was dog-eared. And while I very much admired his courage to rise above the status quo with such contentious ideas, I am still center right on the Mulder/Scully continuum.

But what if it's the nay-sayers that are being close minded? As they say, "absence of proof isn't proof of absence." Let's face it, life can be rather dull. Aliens or intelligent water can add more zest and zeal than a lemon peel. The good news was that Humis and I were on the same page. The bad news? The page we happened to be on was the Table of Contents.

And yet, Professor Humis had a way of piquing my interest and/or curiosity. I wanted to learn more about the unexplainable and inexplicable. Combining hard science with the metaphysical was like a sweet and savory combination of vague obfuscation intermingled with smoke and mirrors. If such sentiment was a trail mix, it wold be composed of honey mustard mini pretzels and chocolate chips. Not bad per se, but odd, in a semi-sweet sort of way. I am still undecided if this new metaphysical course meant we were behind the times or ahead of the times. Was this the stone age or the stoner age?

"THIS IS HARD FOR ME TALK ABOUT, AND JUST AS HARD FOR YOU TO HEAR. AS YOU KNOW ANXIETY RUNS IN YOUR DAD'S SIDE OF THE FAMILY. AND THE MANNER OF DAD'S PASSING FED INTO LYDIA'S PARANOIA."

"MANNER OF DAD'S PASSING?"

"DEREK, LYDIA, AND I WERE VISITING FRIENDS IN KEYSTONE, SOUTH DAKOTA. LYDIA WALKED AROUND A WINDOW-WASHER'S LADDER THAT WAS LEANING AGAINST THE HOTEL."

"DEREK WALKED UNDER IT TO PROVE TO HER HOW SILLY SUCH SUPERSTITIONS WERE. THE VERY NEXT DAY LYDIA FOUND HIM FACE DOWN IN THE HOTEL SWIMMING POOL. LYDIA BLAMED HERSELF FOR HIS DEATH EVER SINCE."

"SHE MAY HAVE BEEN CAPRICIOUS AND PARANOID, BUT IT SOUNDS LIKE HER SUPERSTITIONS CAME TRUE. WHY DIDN'T YOU TELL ME ANY OF THIS?"

"I DIDN'T WANT YOU TO GO DOWN THE SAME RABBIT HOLE YOUR GRANDMA DID."

"I CONVINCED LYDIA TO SEE A THERAPIST. I FOUND A COUNSELOR THAT SPECIALIZED IN GRADUAL EXPOSURE THERAPY, A CERTAIN BRENT BUTLER."

"GRADUAL EXPOSURE? SOUNDS LIKE STRIP POKER."

"ANYWAY, ABOUT TWO MONTHS AFTER YOUR DAD PASSED, BRENT HAD GRANDMA OPEN UP AN UMBRELLA INDOORS."

"A WEEK LATER SHE SLIPPED ON THE STONE STEPS LEADING OUT OF THE THERAPIST'S OFFICE."

"IF I DIDN'T COAX HER INTO GETTING THERAPY SHE MIGHT STILL BE ALIVE TODAY."

"THAT'S NOT YOUR FAULT ANY MORE THAN DAD'S DEATH WAS GRANDMA'S."

"IT'S NOT EASY TO ACCEPT THAT."

"SO DAD AND LYDIA BOTH DIED IN WATER OR ICE RELATED ACCIDENTS AFTER SUPERSTITIOUS ACTIVITIES?"

"DON'T BRING SUPERSTITION INTO THIS. BESIDES, WITH LYDIA THE ACCIDENT HAPPENED A WHOLE WEEK AFTER SHE OPENED THE UMBRELLA. AND HER HEALTH WAS ALREADY GOING DOWNHILL."

"BUT ONLY A WEEK LATER? THAT'S NOT ODD?"

December 25, 2015, 10:15 AM

Dear Diary,

How are you today? Why do I even ask? It's such a one-sided conversation. You should write me back on occasion. Maybe I can threaten you. How about this: if you don't respond soon I will use you as ransom paper. Or I can turn you into a frog using origami like the Frog Prince. If you write back, whether from fear or sheer enjoyment, I might even resume my correspondence using scented resume paper.

I watched a video on YouTube today about cheap hotels. A guy pulled a pillow off the bed and a coterie of cockroaches scattered about. It got me thinking (watch out world). So what did I do? What anyone would do. I tried my best to empathize with a cockroach. To what extent do these "lower life forms" experience fear or pain? Are their faculties more developed than we give them credit for? Are we less intelligent than we give ourselves credit for? My dog Cat seems to understand what I am saying. If only she could speak words back! I wish humans had a stronger connection to our animal brethren. One minute I am watching TV with Cat, almost believing she is human, and the next minute she decides to do "doggy things" like chase her tail or turn multiple circles on the couch before flopping down. Or maybe that wasn't it at all and it was my problem as I just needed to better understand canine culture. But the question remains, if aliens exist, do they make us seem like monkeys in comparison? We hear about bigfoot being the missing link below us. What if aliens are the second missing link above us?

My mind drifted to water science. Do words really have energy and valence? Do our intentions behind the words we say, and the perceptions of the words we receive, contain positive or negative energy? And can water really be affected by this energy? And how do we know if water is imbued with a positive or negative charge? And how far and wide can this charged water affect the surroundings in its wake?

Now on to the subject of Christmas, a subject I have been avoiding, even as I write in this very journal. This morning I opened my eyes to the tune of my mother blasting her Christmas vinyl collection from downstairs as if it were death metal. And to think it was only 8:27 AM in the morning (four seconds into the next minute, to be exact). And I wasn't talking about the jovial and cheery variety of Christmas songs. Or the stupid ones, like "Rockin' Around the Christmas Tree." Or that one about chipmunks and hula hoops. She was playing her more somber and subdued Elvis Christmas album. I zombie-walked to the bottom of the steps and met my mother's gaze. She was sweating over the stove like a blacksmith in an RPG. Her apron was disheveled and covered in waffle batter. Cat was wagging her tail as she watched Mom make the waffles (as if all her labor was for her alone).

I got a Christmas card from my aunt Jenny in Texas. As I was reading, I couldn't help but wonder if she picked up any Southern accent from being there for five years now. Either way my mind gave her one as I read the very letters from her pen. We really should designate "fonts" to denote various accents that correspond with different countries or regions. We could use Chaucer or Allegro for one place and Pegasus for another. And we can't forget Lithograph. Hopefully we can use something more exciting than Arial or Times New Roman. How my thoughts are lately in this diary I should really consider giving myself a nice Cuckoo font. And for mom? Wingdings.

Overall I got a pretty good haul this year for Christmas. I snagged a premiere collector edition Othello, trail mix, and a graphic novel from the same aunt in Texas (not to be confused with the romance variety of graphic novel from the same aunt in Texas (not to be confused with the romance variety of 'graphic novels' my mom reads when I am gone). Still, It sure beats that one time years ago when we were financially struggling, and all I got was an 8-pack of crayons. You know the kind, the ones with the basics: red, green, blue, and orange. Those insufferable aristocrats with their built-in crayon sharpeners and Burnt Sienna!

Some in my position might have felt a modicum of umbrage at the very thought of having their very own mother sign presents as "Santa" in their golden pre-teen years. Truth was, I didn't mind much. I am well aware of memento mori, and I was very inclined to hold on to my youth as long as possible. Only suckers want to grow up!

Less cheery was the magic eight ball (sorry Pac Man & Kirby, the Magic 8-ball was the TRUE pioneer of sentient balls everywhere). Don't get me wrong, mom meant well, but I don't think she realized just how a toy like that might toy with my nervous disposition. As they say, it's the thought that counts. Then again, it's the thoughts that scare me the most.

Can a thought influence random events? I asked the Eight Ball a question about water science. And lo and behold, it spit out the same exact answer three times in a row (the worst answer of the twenty I might add). The odds of the worst answer coming up three times in a row is twenty to the 3rd power, or one in eight thousand. And then my mom shook it to see if the answers might be stuck somehow and not random. But a different answer came up! Did my fear somehow influence the Eight Ball? Was there any cursed water nearby that influenced the answer? Needless to say, a figure eight shape knot formed in my stomach. I no longer felt like a free man, but a victim of fate and circumstance.

People always talk a big game about freedom. But do they even know what it means? All I see are people acting in accordance with how they are expected to act (as sheep in a herd or actors in a play). It's as if they are living in a bird cage with an unlocked (but closed) door. They can see the grassy plains and greener pastures outside the bars from their perch and can leave at any time. But the door may as well be locked, as the shackles of insecurity and conformity prevent them from taking flight. And often they are the first to shame you if you deviate from the beaten path or march to the tune of your own drum. Sometimes I think wisdom has more to do with "unlearning" than "learning." It's about breaking the 4th wall and being aware of all the ways society brainwashes us into mindless robots. It is what it is, as they say. Whose "they" anyway? I don't know for sure. Maybe it's that lot that runs onto tennis courts to retrieve the balls.

I'm not sure if I am in the mood to play Oriello with Jane this weekend. I win most games, and she says I'm a sore winner. I think only sore losers call people sore winners. She says when I eat the cookies in her presence it looks as I am being passive aggressive. Last time we played she had the audacity to say: "You can have your dumb cookies. We had our dirty fingers over them the entire game anyway!"

CHAPTER 5:
DON'T LET IT SNOW,

DON'T LET IT SNOW,

DON'T LET IT SNOW...

2:00 PM.

WAS THIS JUST A SIMPLE CASE OF APOPHENIA? WHY WAS I NOT EVEN IN THE MOOD FOR AMPLE-SAMPLES OF THE WHITMAN'S SAMPLER? NOT EVEN THE "MESSENGER BOY?"

I PREFER TRUFFLES OVER TRIFLES.

AT LEAST I'M NOT THE ONLY ONE. I GUESS HIS GOTH PERSONA AT SCHOOL ISN'T JUST FOR SHOW.

HOW DID JUSTIN MANAGE TO PUT THE FIVE PIECES TOGETHER ON THIS MONSTER?

WOW, CLEVER THAT! IS THAT A SNOW-CENTIPEDE? A SLEETIPEDE?

SECRETIVE MUCH JUSTIN? GARGOYLES AND A BEWARE OF DOG SIGN?

CHALK IT UP TO THE EIGHTH WONDER OF THE WORLD. TIS' A SHAME THAT NOT ALL WONDERS ARE BENEVOLENT.

KIND OF LIKE MIRACLES.

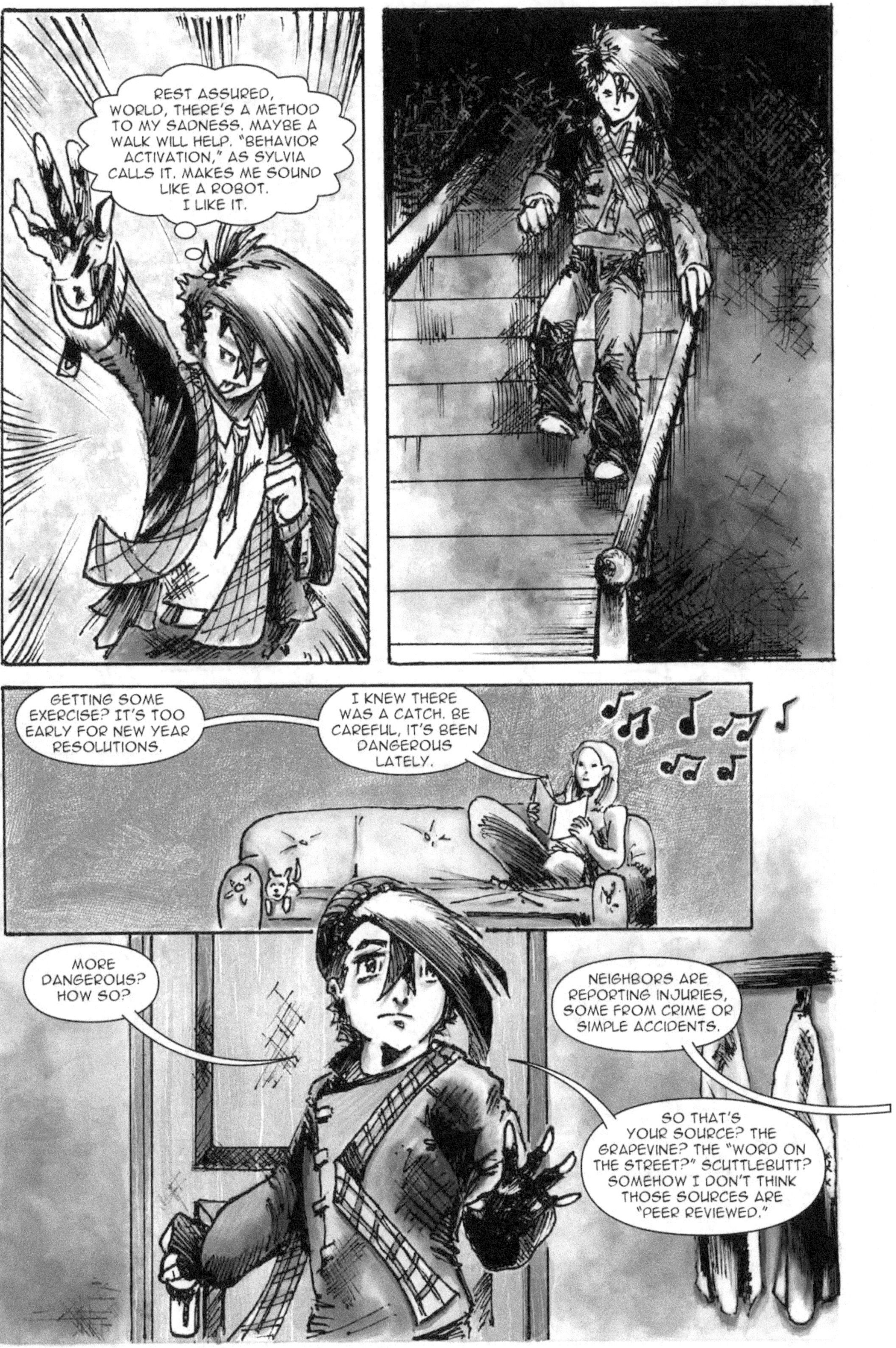

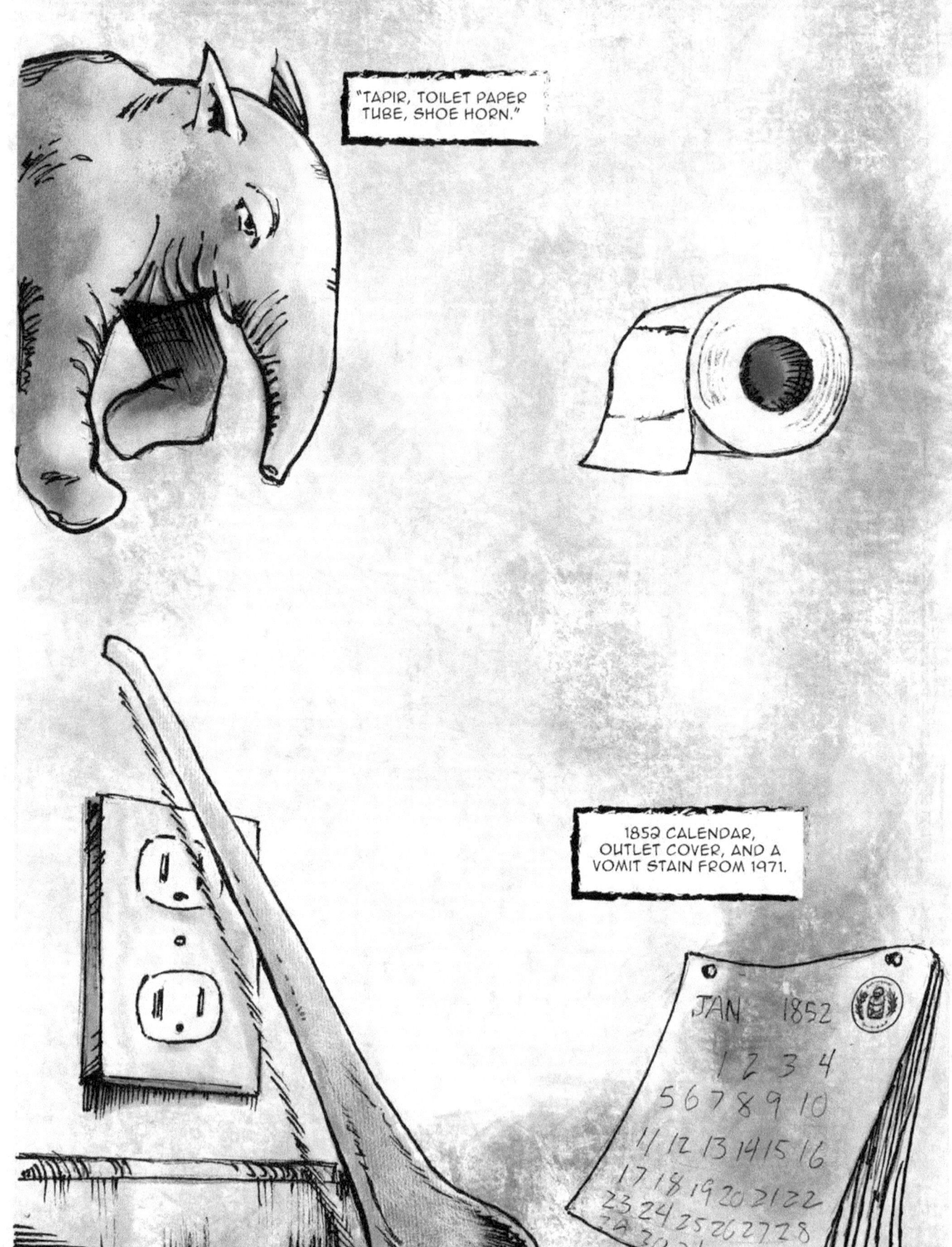

HE SAID THE TORCH REPRESENTS LIBERTY, THE OLIVE BRANCH PEACE, AND THE OAK BRANCH INDEPENDENCE. THESE CONCEPTS MUST BE TOO COMPLEX FOR THE HUMAN RACE.

THE ONLY ONE I FEEL RIGHT NOW IS INDEPENDENCE, BUT THAT'S ONLY BECAUSE I FEEL ALONE.

OKAY TEDDY, FOCUS. TRY THINKING ABOUT TRAVIS HUMIS'S LESSON ON THE U.S. MINT. DO NOT THINK ABOUT ANYTHING SUPERSTITIOUS!

AND TO THINK THOSE WATER DEATHS MY MOTHER MENTIONED ARE JUST THE TIP OF THE ICEBERG, SO TO SPEAK. MAYBE MY GRANDMOTHER REALLY DID PASS THE TORCH TO ME. IF SO, IT SURE DOESN'T FEEL LIKE THE "LIBERTY TORCH" ON THAT DIME.

DID JUSTIN'S PARENTS HELP BUILD THIS SLEETIPEDE? THOSE BRANCHES FOR ITS LEGS ARE NOT LIKE THE OLIVE BRANCHES ON THAT DIME EITHER.

AND BEWARE OF DOG? DO THEY EVEN HAVE A DOG? MAYBE THAT SIGN IS A DIFFERENT TAKE ON HAVING A FAKE CAMERA.

SO I GET INTO AN ACCIDENT THE VERY MOMENT I STEP INTO THE FORBIDDEN ZONE.

DID JUSTIN USE WATER SCIENCE ON THE SNOW DURING CHRISTMAS BREAK?

WAS THE SNOW CURSED BY THE GARGOYLES? DID I GIVE THE SNOW BAD VIBES WHEN I TRESPASSED ON THE BANNERS' PROPERTY?

"LATER ON, WE'LL CONSPIRE, AS WE DREAM BY THE FIRE, TO FACE UNAFRAID, PLANS THAT WE'VE MADE, WALKING IN A WINTER WONDERLAND."

WHAT HAPPENED TO ME WAS JUST LIKE WHAT HAPPENED TO GRANDMA WHEN SHE SLIPPED ON THE ICY STEPS A SCANT WEEK AFTER THE THERAPIST MADE HER OPEN AN UMBRELLA INDOORS.

HOME IS WHERE THE HEART IS

I KNOW HOW YOU FEEL, DOORMAT. ALTHOUGH I CAN'T FOR THE LIFE OF ME UNDERSTAND HOW YOU CAN REMAIN SO POSITIVE AFTER BEING WALKED OVER BY SO MANY PEOPLE.

MAYBE IT'S TIME TO OPEN WHITMAN'S BOX. I ALREADY OPENED PANDORA'S. LIFE IS MOST CERTAINLY NOT LIKE A BOX OF CHOCOLATES. AT LEAST THE CANDY GUIDE INSIDE THE LID LETS YOU KNOW WHAT YOU ARE IN FOR.

December 25, 2015

Dear Diary,

Here I am, pensive with a pen, sitting at my diary as if it was a sacred tome, shrine, or Macguffin in some adventure story. And to think I never used to even write in a diary until I started seeing my school counselor (now Sylvia Koch as she was just married two weeks ago). She encouraged me to journal each and every day as a coping skill (although my ink-laden proliferation has been a bit more macabre than the "gratitude statements" she has been wanting me to write as of late).

It's only about 5:30 pm, a bit early for writing, but I figured I needed ample opportunity to transcribe my angsty elucidation from pen to parchment. And with my trepidation from my already superstitious disposition there are times when it feels like it's not my hand that guides the pen but rather my pen that guides the hand. All this business with the Magic Eight Ball and Water Science has put me in a sort of existential frenzy and/or tizzy (whichever came first).

I should never have taken that brisk jaunt to Justin Banner's. Those gargoyles should have been my first warning. And the sleetipede snowcrow should have been the second (at least now I know how crows feel). The "Beware of dog" sign should have been my third and final cue (I guess Jane was right that I can't take a hint). Maybe if they had a junkyard dog that trap would have caught him instead of me. At least nobody saw the serious accident (despite my shouting like a drill-sergeant). I must have looked (and felt) like David when he dropped that heavy microphone on his foot during his "Why I Chose Academy Anomaly" speech at last year's career fair. Talk about a "mic drop" moment. I guess not all mic drops end on a high note.

I didn't have many options. All I could do was turn around, put my large candy cane to the ground, and hobble back home like a lock-step soldier (instead of a drill sergeant). If only this soldier had a field hospital. It was ironic how that sleetipede, the object of nightmares, was able to help me walk home using his candy-cane antennae. Maybe I should thank him. Then again, maybe that sleetipede just had a bad case of "Munchausen by Proxy" and set the trap there himself. At least my thievery had good intentions. Just like Robin Hood.

After what seemed like two hours of hobbling, I reached my not-so-humble abode (no small feat when you have a zombie-like gait). The "Home is Where the Heart Is" doormat below my feet made a mighty bold claim (I am still waiting for scientists to prove it). Or maybe I am misinterpreting it and it's alluding to something a bit more literal, something like a nefarious basement black market heart-donor trade. Make no mistake, I am not having a go at basement dwellers (that would be abasement). I am one of them, after all.

The Christmas lights above me lost their Christmas cheer. and may as well have been a prison spotlight. The last thing I needed was to call attention to my mom's watchful gaze, which was more responsive and aware than Sauron's eye. These lights were the old kind, the ones that won't light up if there is a single bad bulb in the bunch. In cartoons a lightbulb above your head represents a thought or some sort of epiphany. I had an epiphany all right, but it wasn't the yule tide variety. My "aha" moment was akin to something of a more paranoid persuasion. I wished the bulb above my head would have just burned out, taking the entire string of Christmas lights along with it. There was no doubt about it, my zest and zeal for my favorite day of the year came to an abrupt end. Good thing it wasn't mistletoe (although my toe felt like it was hit by a ballistic).

But I must confess, it wasn't very Christmas-like to steal that large plastic candy cane (or for trespassing in Justin's yard for that matter). I guess I am now a thief (just not a common one). There are now footprints all over the place. If they trace them back to my Sorel boots I am screwed. It would be like Cinderella but without the happy ending.

After all that drama, I needed some chocolate therapy (yet to be recognized as an evidenced-based practice). And I wasn't about to settle for "fun size" (what's so fun about less candy?). And sitting here in the aftermath of it all, right here and now, I have a "confectionery confession" to make. I ate half the box of Whitman's Sampler as evidenced by the little papers strewn all over my bed as if a bed of roses. I started with the Messenger Boy (so much for "don't murder the messenger.") It was more like "death by chocolate."

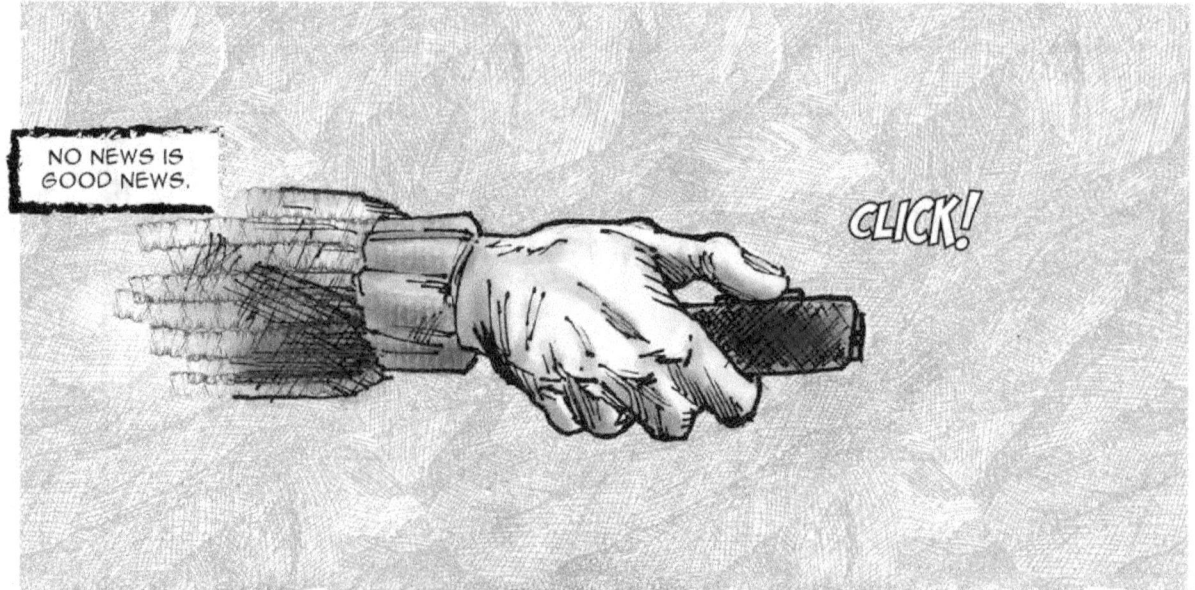

NO NEWS IS GOOD NEWS.

CLICK!

SYLVIA MENTIONED MAKING A PROS AND CONS LIST WHEN FACING A TOUGH DECISION. I THINK SHE CALLED IT A DECISIONAL BALANCE SHEET.

"SUSTAINS LIFE, VARIOUS APPLICATIONS IN SOLID, LIQUID, OR STEAM STATES CAN DRINK IT, SHOWER WITH IT, OR COOK WITH IT, CAN KEEP THINGS COOL WITH ICE, CAN CLEAN WITH IT, URINATION AND IRRIGATION, WATER BALLOONS AND SQUIRT GUNS, HOT CHOCOLATE, SNOW DAYS."

BENEFITS OF WATER

"CAN DROWN IN IT, MIGHT SLIP ON IT, FLOODING, BLIZZARDS, OR HAIL DAMAGE, MIGHT EXACERBATE MOLD GROWTH..."

CONS OF WATER

"FREEZER BURN, FROSTBITE OR HYPOTHERMIA, MIGHT CONTAIN CONTAMINANTS, DOESN'T TASTE AS GOOD AS POP."

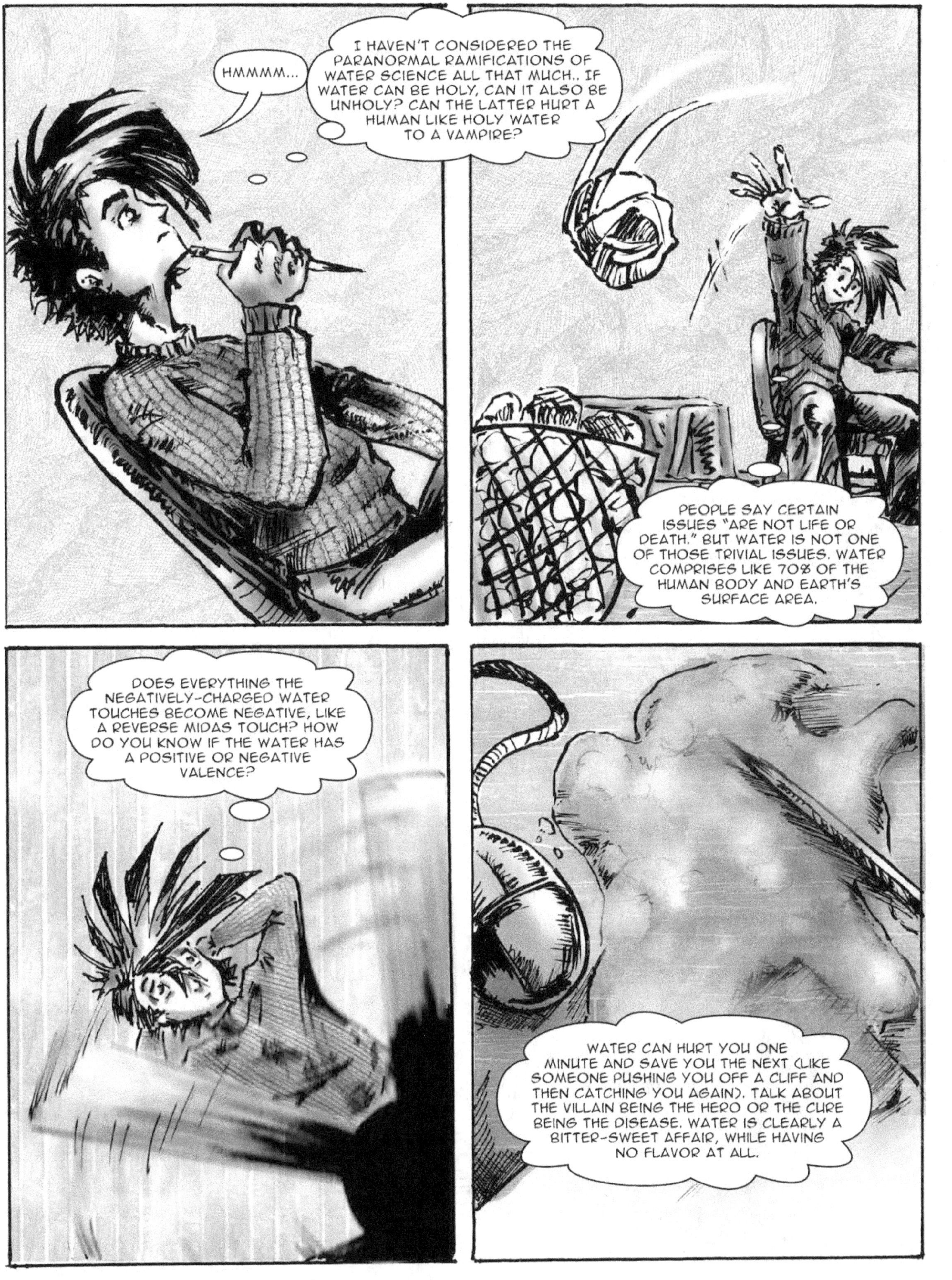

December 25, 2015

Dear Diary,

This is my second time at my diary today! On Christmas no less! What gives? This has gotta be the first time all year when I wrote two entries in a single day. So what's the reason for the treason? I'm afraid it's my confounded superstitious disposition. The wherefore and why of the why and the wherefore. The very mysteries of life and death itself! And yet they say "don't sweat the small stuff." It's too bad I can't tell the difference between the "small stuff" and the "big stuff." I don't know why I bother writing to you, Dear Diary. You always give me the silent treatment.

This was a rather lackluster Christmas. But it's not over yet! I still have four hours left. Maybe I should keep traveling west into different time zones and extend the day in hopes to make it better. If I can get to Alaska, I could free up another three hours! But do I even need to physically exist in Alaska before I am "allowed" to use Alaska time? Could I adopt it right now, as my own personal cultural preference? I give myself the right! I hereby declare, right here and now, that it is not 8pm as my clock asserts. It is 5pm, Alaska time! I have 7 hours of Christmas left! Then again, Christmas might have three additional hours to dish out more bad luck. Maybe I should fly East instead.

Mom said that the mailman (Mr. Wellington) wants to interview me soon to help deliver papers on days when the roads are too icy to drive on. After what I saw on the news earlier today I can't see why anyone even bothers getting the paper in the first place. They must be gluttons for punishment. Besides, job interviews are just personality tests in disguise (as these employers already know your credentials). The interview is just to assess the "sunniness" of your disposition. Small wonder they call employees human resources" (as if humans were the stuff of coal, lignite, or tungsten). There are only two other groups of people that talk about "human resources," and they are cannibals & vampires.

During supper mom was talking about how her outdoorsy friend Mandy invited her to go "bow hunting" on New Year's Eve. I tried picturing her in camouflage with war paint under her eyes (something like Katnis Everdeen). Then again, maybe Mandy meant "beau hunting," as in the barefoot and bashful variety. You know the type, a husband hunter. A panther. A siren! Although in all honesty, I didn't believe that either. And neither did she. We both knew full well that nobody could replace my dad.

Just before I put pen to paper on this diary entry, I was staring out the window at the large lighted Christmas tree outside. And two seconds after I was staring at it the lights went out! Either my mother had unplugged them or one of the lights must have burned out and affected the whole string. At least that was my string-theory.

And all this business with those lights just got me thinking about the old traffic light across the street (now displaying a candle Christmas ornament that the City erected). That traffic light has been a fixture near my house for as long as I can remember. I wonder how many times the light has changed in the last forty years? And to think that for every time the light changes from green to yellow to red people are like rats in a maze going in difference directions, each with their own agenda and employments. I would love to meet all the drivers that were at the very intersection when the light turned red for the seventh time on the day of March 7, 1991. I wonder where they were going and what they are all doing now. It's not as if any one of them would remember that moment they stopped at that very light on that very day at that very time. And that is just one lonely traffic light. What about every other traffic light, in every city, state, country, and world? Street lights highlight an impasse, where people get in each other's way, if only for a moment, as they embark on their own journeys to find gold at the end of their personal rainbows.

It is now about 9:00 pm as I sit at my diary, or 6pm Alaska time. I have done my fair share of researching testimonials, books, and websites about all manner of water. Should I do another rice experiment? Nah, those are a dime a dozen. I need something a little different, novel, and otherwise newsworthy.

I will start planning tomorrow. I don't have any expectations of what the results will be. That's probably for the best, as a true scientist really shouldn't have any emotional investment one way or the other. In fact, if I had it my way there would be a science journal dedicated to publishing studies that did NOT show significant results. After all, isn't it just as important to know what doesn't work in addition to what does? Why should "significant" studies be any more useful than the ones that aren't? It appears that even science has fell by the wayside along with the likes of tabloids and the hoi polloi.

Science Journal, Water Experiment Setup

December 26, 2015

Overview of experiment:

Phase 1 of experiment
    I will use all three of the closets in my house to make this experiment work (and to avoid confounds). One closet will be the control group, and the other two the treatment groups. The first priority will be to use my dehumidifier in each closet to extract water from the air and capture enough water to fill up three mayo jars. Thankfully I can use my extensive collection of mobile phones that I have accumulated over time for the experiment as well, since I can still use their voice recording features offline. Not only that, but I figure it will be a more controlled study if I play the recordings in each closet simultaneously to rule out any time-order influences. The three closets are quite distant from each other so they shouldn't pick up any extraneous signals from the other closets. I aim to have fifteen minutes of recorded speech in each of the three conditions. I will place one phone in each of the three closets and let them do their thing. One phone will play my own voice saying compliments, another will play my voice saying insults, and the third phone will display neutral monotone statements. This will give the water inside each jar a negative, positive, or neutral valence.
    The emotions behind the words will have to be genuine, and spoken in a very sincere manner. And whatever objects I decide to place into each jar of water will need to be have the same mass (to two decimal places). One can only hope that the closets will shield the air and water from any household dysfunction that might (undoubtedly) occur.

1. Control Group (neutral energy): For this condition, I will record myself

saying fifteen minutes worth of neutral statements spoken with a monotone voice using flat emotion.
Each statement will have three words. I will say: " grass is green," " curtains get dusty," and " paper is thin." The jar of water in closet number one will receive this treatment.

2. Treatment group 1 (negative energy): For this condition I will record myself saying fifteen minutes worth of negative statements, spoken with volume and genuine angst. This shouldn't be too hard, as even Sylvia knows about my negative self talk. I will say things such as: "you don't deserve to live," " nobody likes you," or " why did dad have to die." The jar of water in closet number two will receive this treatment.

3. Treatment group 2 (positive energy): For this condition, I will record myself saying fifteen minutes worth of positive comments spoken with conviction and a joyful voice and excited emotion. I will say things such as: " I'm grateful to have Jane as a friend," " At least I still have my mom," and " Professor Humis is someone I look up to." The jar of water in closet number three will receive this treatment.

Phase two of experiment:
The day after Phase 1 the experiment will take on a more interesting tone. After having my three jars of water, I will need three red roses from the local Country Greenery. They will need to be of a similar age and appearance. I decided on roses because I thought maybe I could achieve quicker results than I could with rice. I will put all three vases on my dresser in my room (being careful not to confound the results in any way as the roses are left alone (at least whatever happens in my room will affect all three roses, reducing confounds). And then comes the fun part. I will watch and observe over the next few days or so, taking copious notes about the roses' development and/or decline.

Science Journal: Results of Water Experiment

New Year's Day, January 1, 2016

I finished my experiment, and on New Year's no less. By now all three roses were pretty much not pretty. The most notable of my findings were on day four. The rose in the "negative vase" really did seem more wilted and disheveled than the other two roses. Likewise the rose in the "positive vase" appeared more hale and hearty than the one in the "negative treatment" group. I took pictures with my phone to get a visual on the evidence (I even touched and smelled the evidence). I took photos and notes of the "positive water" rose as before, along with my more subjective tactile and olfactory tests. The rose in the control group was a different matter. It did not look all that much worse for wear than the flower in the positive vase. In fact, it looked and smelled slightly better.

So far the results of my experiment produced at least some credence for the proponents of water science. After day four, the roses became more and more similar in appearance as they all began to rot and spoil. And they all smelled just as putrid. I continued to take pictures and copious notes of the roses. I also put my new microscope to use and analyzed collected samples of water from each vase. I was able to use the microscopes built-in camera to take pictures of each slide. Sure enough, the water in the "negative" condition did produce more bacteria than the other two vases. The evidence from the slides seemed to further provide evidence for the proponents of water science. This lended support for their alternate hypothesis. As for me? This time I was rooting for the null hypothesis.

In the end, my results were more bitter than sweet. (80% bitter vs. 20% sweet on the bitter-sweet continuum). This did precious little to quell my nervous disposition (I was feeling even more hypervigilant and paranoid, and I even developed a physical tremor in my hands). I had no choice but to admit it. There seemed to be truth to water science after all, and all those nasty events as of late were in fact caused by water with a " negative charge." At the very least, at least someone sent me flowers.

DEREK JALES, DIED NOVEMBER 8, 2014. DEREK HELD A REWARDING AND LENGTHY CAREER AS A RESEARCH PSYCHOLOGIST FOR THE MINNEAPOLIS PSYCHOLOGY PROJECT (SPECIALIZING IN THE STUDY OF PERSONALITY AND SOCIAL PSYCHOLOGY AND HOW THEY RELATE TO CHARITABLE OR ALTRUISTIC BEHAVIORS). HE WAS HIGHLY REGARDED BY HIS PEERS, AND HE HELD THE SAME POSITION FOR OVER TWENTY YEARS (ONE OF THE LABS WAS NAMED AFTER HIM IN 2009). ONE OF HIS MAJOR CONTRIBUTIONS WAS DISCOVERING HOW FEAR OF PAIN OR ANTICIPATION OF REWARD CAN INFLUENCE ACTS OF ALTRUISM. HE ALSO COACHED THE DEBATE TEAM AT ANOMALY ACADEMY MIDDLE SCHOOL. HE ENJOYED SCRAP-BOOKING AND READING NON-FICTION. DEREK JALES IS SURVIVED BY HIS WIFE KAREN AND SON THEODORE.

LYDIA JALES, DIED DECEMBER 18, 2014. FOR OVER THIRTY YEARS LYDIA WORKED AS A CERTIFIED TAX PREPARER AND WOULD PREPARE TAXES FOR FREE FOR THOSE WITH LIMITED INCOMES. EVERY YEAR ON CHRISTMAS SHE ALSO DONATED HER TIME AT THE SOUP KITCHEN AT THE COMPASSION MISSION HOMELESS SHELTER. SHE ENJOYED QUILTING AND PLAYING HORSE SHOES. LYDIA JALES IS SURVIVED BY HER GRANDSON THEODORE AND DAUGHTER-IN-LAW KAREN.

CHAPTER 7:
DAYDREAMS AND/OR NIGHTMARES

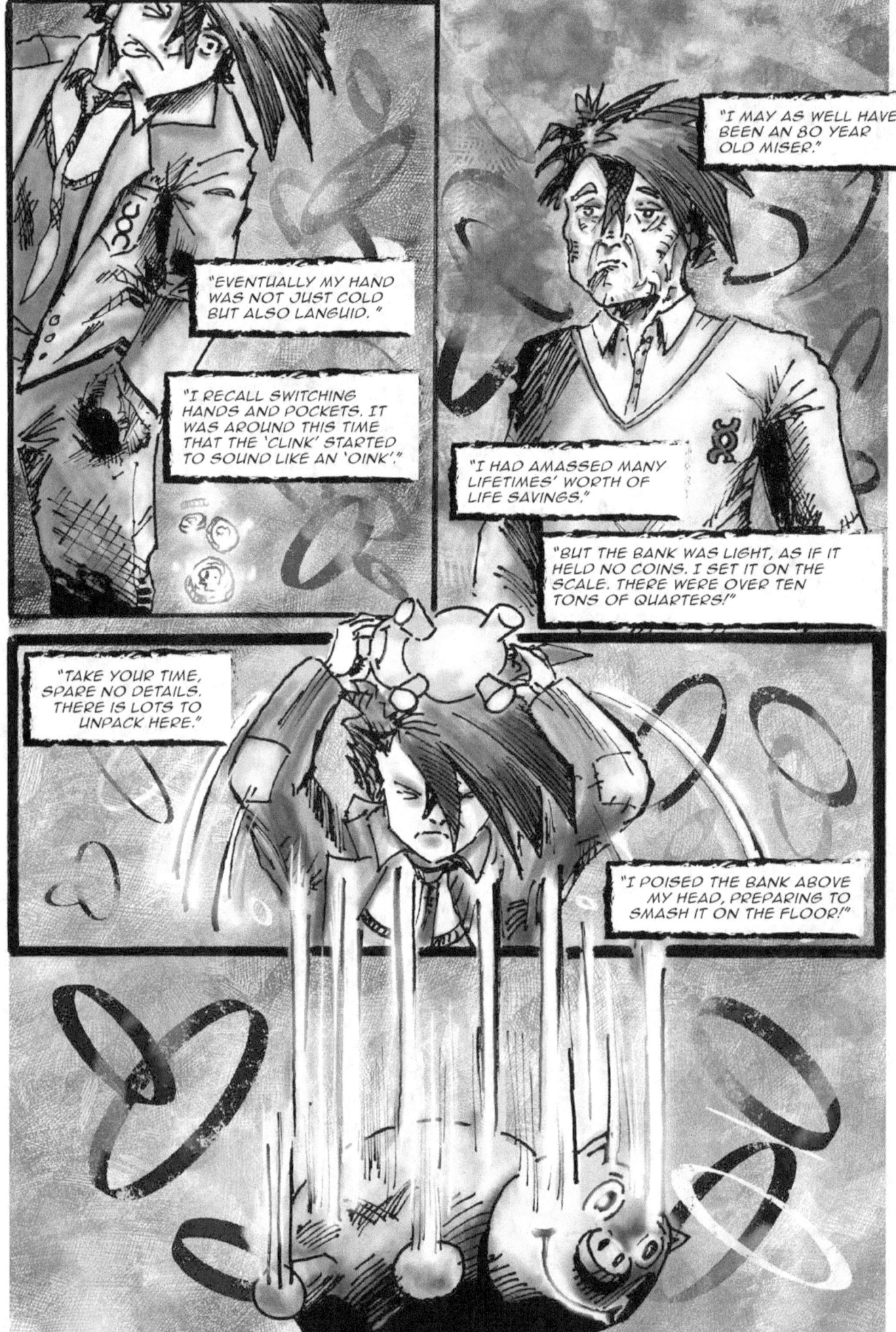

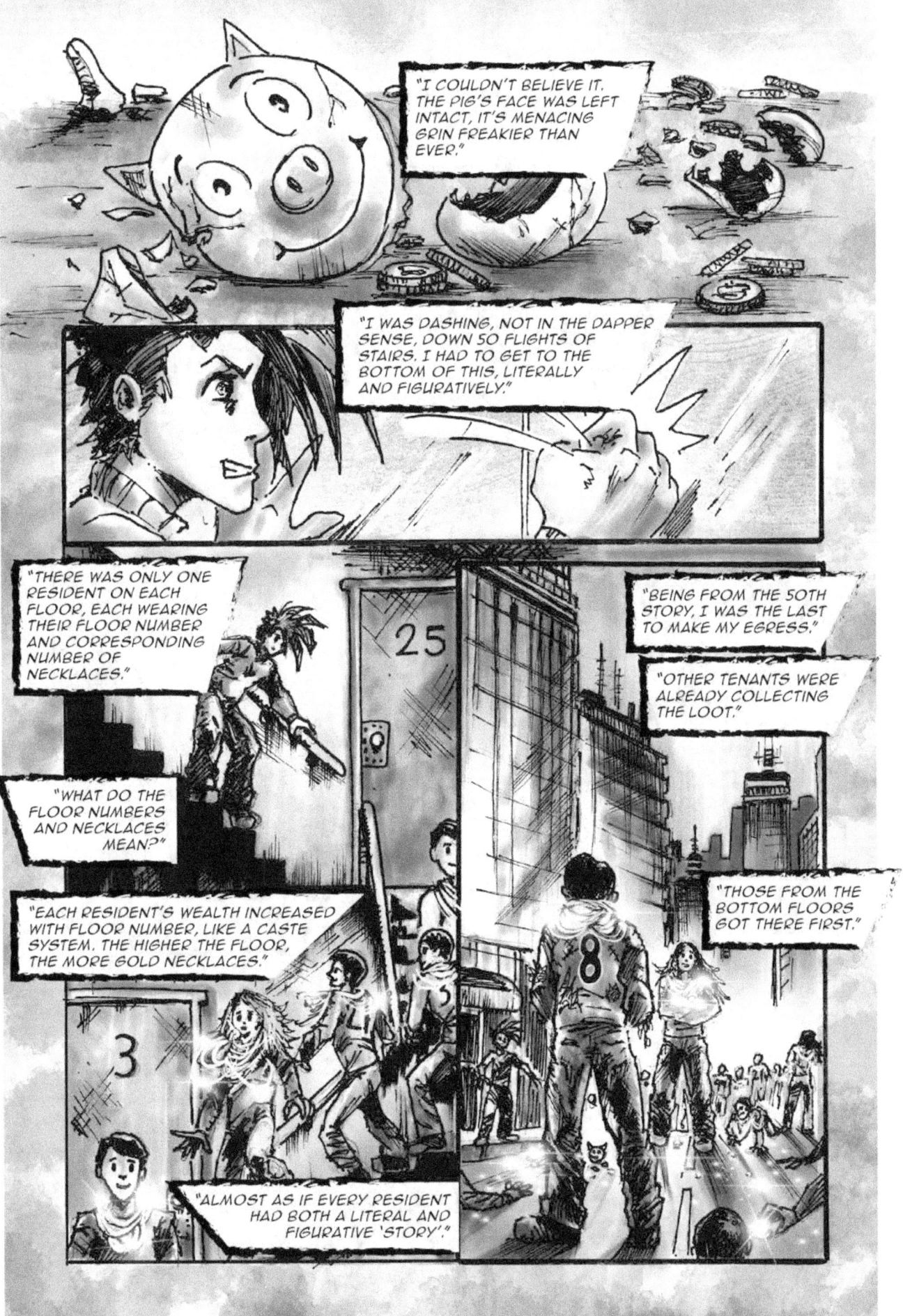

January 25, 2016

Dear Diary,

I saw Sylvia this morning. I'm still not sure how genuine she is. But I give Sylvia mad props for sharing how she got over her bee phobia through dream analyses. At least it made her seem like she had a semblance of humanity. If this was an RPG or RTS, our "rapport score" would have went up 3 points after that. Before our session expired I asked her if she felt ready to get near a bee to prove she was over her fears. She replied: "Well, I wouldn't want to be alone with one if that is what you mean!" I asked, "how about two?" She turned the topic back to my dream! Now whose deflecting?

I spent part of my session asking Sylvia why so many punishments didn't seem to befit the crime in the criminal justice system. There are often situations where a twenty second crime translates into a twenty year sentence! Either people love vigilante justice or they suck at math. Pain and pleasure should really be measured by their duration, frequency, and intensity. Sylvia said it's because people think with their emotions and what "feels right" instead of approaching it like a math problem. She added that crime and punishment is also like an "industry" of sorts with a business element to it. All I know is that in regards to "deterrence theory" (and animal training for that matter) behavior is more likely to be modified if the reward is immediate (celerity), consistent (certainty), and with sufficient intensity (seriousness). If only people would get pulled over randomly for obeying the speed limit and get a cash reward instead. There should really also be a discount for telling the truth.

I don't know why I feel bad for so-called "bad people." The only thing separating me from them is a simple roll of the dice. It's not like I'm a pillar of virtue.

Other students call Sylvia a cat lady but she only has one cat. How many cats do you need before you can be Christened as a cat lady?

I can't say for sure, but if it only takes one then I guess that makes me a "dog man" since I have a dog (named Cat). But somehow I don't think "dog man" is going to make its way into colloquial vernacular. But I like the sound of "dog man." It has a nice ring to it. And it makes me sound like a werewolf.

    I told her all about my nightmare, and she got all Freudian and asked me to think about what the various themes might mean. She asked me if the 50 story building divided by class had anything to do with "attending class" or "class warfare" at Anomaly academy. After all, elementary school was like the lower class, middle school the middle class, and high school the higher class. In this context, "class" had less to do with "money" and more to do with "grade" and "status." Sylvia further theorized that maybe my dream had something to do with going to high school next year in a new building across town. But then after all that supposed dream analyses she gave up and said "sometimes a dream is just a dream." And "consequently" that is just when we "ran out of time." Talk about a cop-out! Freud would have flunked her for sure. Can I trust that woman? Sylvia can sure be a real piece of work, and I don't mean "The Scream" by Edvard Munch.

    My homework for next Monday was to think about the style of trauma responses and "avoidant behaviors" I used on a regular basis. When I asked, "you mean fight vs. flight?" she said there were not three but four now: fight, flight, freeze, and fawn. This made me livid! How dare they ruin the cute little rhyme scheme they had going with adding two words that didn't even rhyme with "fight" or "flight?" I get it, they still start with "F." But who cares! Consonance is no substitute for a good rhyme! I proffered the idea of maintaining the rhyme by substituting "freeze" with "fright." I still don't know what to replace "fawn" with. The best I could come up was the verb form of "delight" (as in appease, pacify, or make happy). Still, Sylvia reminded me to spend less time on the pedantic matters and more time on the purpose of the exercise (to think about the unhealthy ways I avoid my trauma triggers under the guise of "coping skills"). She said I was neurodivergent and had the audacity to say that I was also a HSP. I asked what HSP stood for and she said "highly sensitive person." I took offense at this accusation and told her that it sounded rather insulting. And what did she say? She told me not to be so sensitive!

LOW RISK PLANS TEND TO HAVE A HIGH PREMIUM AND LOW DEDUCTIBLE. HIGH RISK PLANS OFTEN HAVE A LOW PREMIUM BUT HIGH DEDUCTIBLE.

YOU MAKE IT SOUND LIKE LAS VEGAS. LET'S JUST HOPE THE HOUSE DOESN'T ALWAYS WIN.

"REMINDS ME OF THE COUNTY FAIR. THOSE BIG TEDDY BEARS ARE JUST FOR SHOW. INSURANCE PRIZES ARE LESS CUTE AND CUDDLY. WINNING THIS GAME MIGHT SCORE YOU A SHINY NEW PROSTHETIC ARM."

BUT THIS PLAN IS INTERESTING AS IT HAS A LOW PREMIUM AND A LOW DEDUCTIBLE.

AND IT'S GOT SPECIFIC ADD-ON OPTIONS FOR ARM, LEG, HEAD, OR NECK INJURIES. IT LOOKS PRETTY LEGIT TO ME.

I SCOURED THE FINE PRINT AS WELL. NOTHING STOOD OUT TO ME.

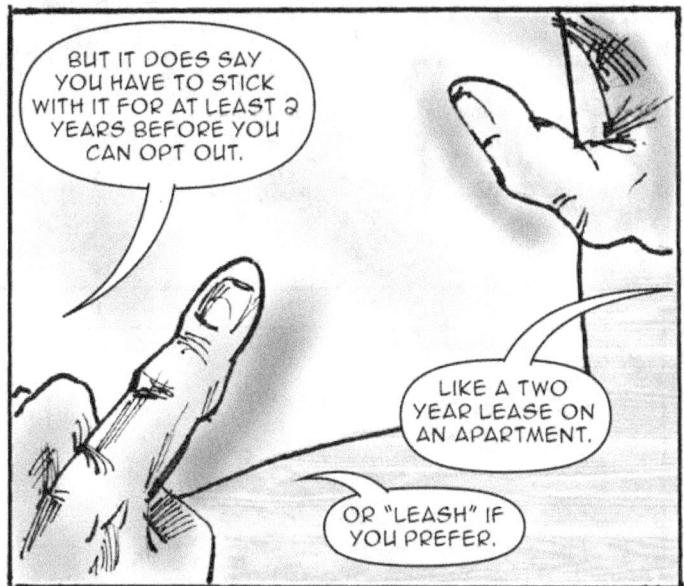

BUT IT DOES SAY YOU HAVE TO STICK WITH IT FOR AT LEAST 2 YEARS BEFORE YOU CAN OPT OUT.

LIKE A TWO YEAR LEASE ON AN APARTMENT.

OR "LEASH" IF YOU PREFER.

GOTTA LOVE HOW THESE BROCHURES ALWAYS SHOW PEOPLE ALL GIDDY ABOUT HAVING THEIR MEDICAL BILLS PAID FOR AS IF THEY WON A TRIP TO DISNEYLAND.

THESE COMPANIES USE SOPHISTICATED STATISTICS TO PREDICT WHEN PEOPLE ARE GOING TO DIE.

FAMILY

SHIT! I SPILLED THE BAD RICE WATER ON THE FORMS!

QUICK, GET SOME TOWELS! I WILL MOVE THE JARS OUT OF THE WAY.

I HOPE THESE PAPERS DRY. HUMIS SURE SPENT LOTS OF TIME WORKING ON THEM. WHERE DID HE GO?

YOU KNOW THAT SNOWMAN BY THE FIRE HYDRANT?

THE ONE THAT LOOKS READY TO ROB A SNOW BANK, FREEZE FUNDS, LIQUIDATE ASSETS, AND STEAL SLUSH FUNDS?

THAT'S THE ONE! I EMPTIED THE JAR OF EVIL RICE WATER ON THE SNOWMAN'S HEAD!

TELL ME YOU DIDN'T. QUICK, WE GOTTA DESTROY THAT SNOWMAN!

DON'T YOU DARE!

THE THIRD GRADERS MADE THAT SNOWMAN DURING THEIR ART CLASS BEFORE CHRISTMAS.

WHAT'S THE ISSUE, TEDDY? CAN I TRUST YOU NOT TO SMASH THIS SNOWMAN TO BITS?

I WON'T HURT THE SNOWMAN. EVEN SCROOGE HIMSELF WOULDN'T BE SO CAVALIER. BUT I WISH YOU HADN'T DONE THAT.

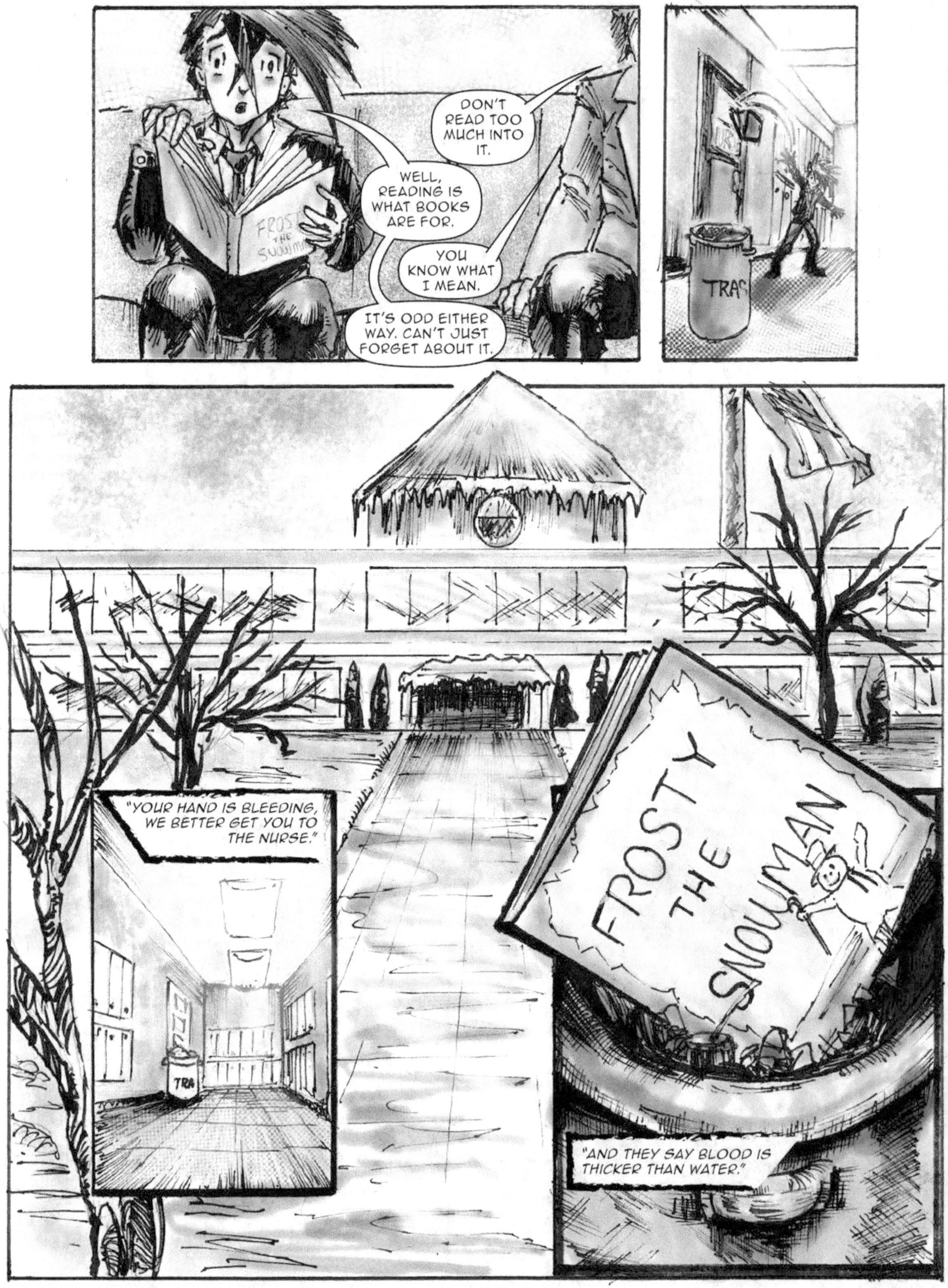

DON'T READ TOO MUCH INTO IT.

WELL, READING IS WHAT BOOKS ARE FOR.

YOU KNOW WHAT I MEAN.

IT'S ODD EITHER WAY. CAN'T JUST FORGET ABOUT IT.

"YOUR HAND IS BLEEDING, WE BETTER GET YOU TO THE NURSE."

FROSTY THE SNOWMAN

"AND THEY SAY BLOOD IS THICKER THAN WATER."

January 26, 2016 (Tuesday)

Dear Diary,

I am sitting at my writing desk, listening to my anime soundtracks. Spice and Wolf to be exact. And Death Note is on the docket. I took a moment to handle the jewel cases. I couldn't help but realize how the overall experience wasn't just about the music. Physical media is a multi-sensory experience. It's the visual vibes of the insert, the font of the song titles, the order of the songs, the placement of the pictures, and even the smell of the booklet itself (I didn't do a taste test). And this is perhaps even more relevant now, during the decline and obsolescence of physical media. After all, CD's have reached their Apex and zenith in the 1990's.

Why do people brag about being "young and hip" as if it was some talent or skill-set? It's not so funny when the time comes when they hit their own twilight years. They just get teased by their own kids and the "cycle continues" (just like a spinning CD). And the same can be said for their hubris surrounding their "cutting edge technology." cowboys sent text messages using the telegraph back in the 1800's. And the Polaroid could take selfies since the 40's.

Now Mr. Diary, I have a question for you, and I assure you it's not rhetorical. If one forgets to mark spills with a warning sign, and someone falls, who is truly culpable for such malfeasance? The person who wasn't cognizant of the environment? Or the person who failed to put out the warning sign? Or a combination of both? I suppose there are hundreds of factors at play, each one being semi-responsible or relevant in its own way (even the manufacturer of the warning sign itself). And yet, we try to pigeon-hole culpability into only two categories of innocent and guilty or good vs. evil. I guess that's why the torch and pitchfork community prefers politics over science. All that "emotional reasoning" Sylvia was talking about yesterday. And that's also why I prefer science over politics. Who am I kidding. Why am I asking you? It's not as if you will ever answer back. You are just like

Sylvia, and all your answers are just more questions. "How does that make you feel?" Not good!

When a natural disaster happens (such as when Mt. Vesuvius covered Pompeii), we acknowledge the science behind it (after all, volcanos erupt for a reason). When people do things that hurt others, however, people make it seem as if the rules of causality go out the window. Is there really a difference between the two? Don't all things happen for a reason in the natural world? Rest assured this question is also not rhetorical

Jane texted me after school and asked me if I had a ruler she could borrow, as she wanted to measure her plants she was watering for her rice experiments. I told her there wasn't a Russian Czar residing at my house if that's what she meant. She said I was being a smart alec. I told her laughter was the best medicine. And to that she retorted, "well yes, but you should laugh with me, not at me." I just replied" they just said laughter, they didn't specify what kind." And what did she do? She sent me an emoji (the one with the steam coming out of the nose). And it wasn't because she just ate a hot pepper.

When Jane and I made our amends over the phone, we talked about the pros and cons of dress codes at Anomaly Academy. She was not in favor of them as they impeded individuality of appearance and promoted lock-step conformity. My stance was that despite all my non-conformist punk rock sensibilities, dress codes are nice as everyone is treated as equals. We are freed from the dog-eat-dog world of name brand fashion, pecking order, status-seeking, and other skullduggery. I reminded her that individuality is one thing, and showing off is quite another. She asked me if I would be a showoff if we didn't have dress codes. I told her I would wear a Zoloft shirt to brag about how I had something that was name brand for once (and not the generic Sertraline HCL). And what did she say? She said it would be a brazen boast, as not everything name-brand will boost one's status (and might even have the opposite effect). I think she takes the opposite stance on things just to ruffle my feathers. Jane can sure be a "piece of work," and I don't mean Van Gogh's "The Starry Night."

Today Professor Humis asked me to help him choose a new insurance plan called Pygmalion. I didn't say anything at the time, but I felt flattered that he asked me of all people. I read the fine print myself, and it all seemed innocuous enough (well, as innocuous as an insurance company can be). From what I could tell, Pygmalion insurance seemed above board. Let's just hope this "board" isn't the kind pirates use when they make you walk the plank.

Speaking of Professor Humis, he emptied the "bad vibes" rice and water concoction atop the snowman's head at school today. I noticed that the spot where David punched his midsection was still visible. I slipped near the snowman less than five minutes later, and it reminded me about how I also stepped on that animal trap near the sleetipede over at Justin Banner's place. Were these two snowmen imbued with dark energy? Don't get me wrong, Albert Einstein was one of my idols (one of his name's famous anagrams happens to be "ten elite brains"). If only E=MC (squared) factored in light and dark energy. And if only we had an eleventh elite brain to figure that one out. I don't know if "Heady Teddy" is up to the task.

And then when we went back inside the school, I saw what appeared to be a brand new children's book, Frosty the Snowman, sitting in the garbage can plain as day. It wasn't even Christmas time. And why would such a book be in middle school and not elementary? I was reluctant to reach my hands into the disgusting garbage can, but my confounded superstitions from recent events trumped my fear of germs (lesser of two evils). I reached in like a fisherman hand-fishing for a catfish. I flipped through it so fast I tore a few pages. And lo and behold, the book was missing the pages covering the part of the story where Frosty dies!! How could anyone not find this odd? And it wasn't the good kind of odd, like the fact that Oscar the Grouch used to be orange. It was a more ominous variety, a justified sense of danger that I could not explain away using Sylvia's cozy reality checks and cognitive restructuring. Was there a connection between the book to Christmas a month ago when my mother's record skipped on that very part of the story? If only my school nurse could break this spell or stop uncanny bad luck dead in its tracks. Then again, even if she was such a miracle worker, she still had the bedside manner of a bedbug.

It is about a quarter past seven in the evening right now as I am writing, and I hear knocking on the main door downstairs. It was none other than my nasty grandfather on my dad's side, Clint Jales. I just mumbled that trite one-liner they say in every action movie: "Oh no, we got company." If only my mom's in-laws weren't out-laws.

The more I think about it the more anxious I get. If only this diary could show the look on my face at this very moment. Only a polaroid could capture this level of paranoid. There is one thing that Frosty the Snowman book and this diary have in common. You can't judge a book by its cover. And if there is one thing I have learned, you can't judge a cover by its book either.

CHAPTER 9:
A SNOWBALL'S CHANCE IN HELL...

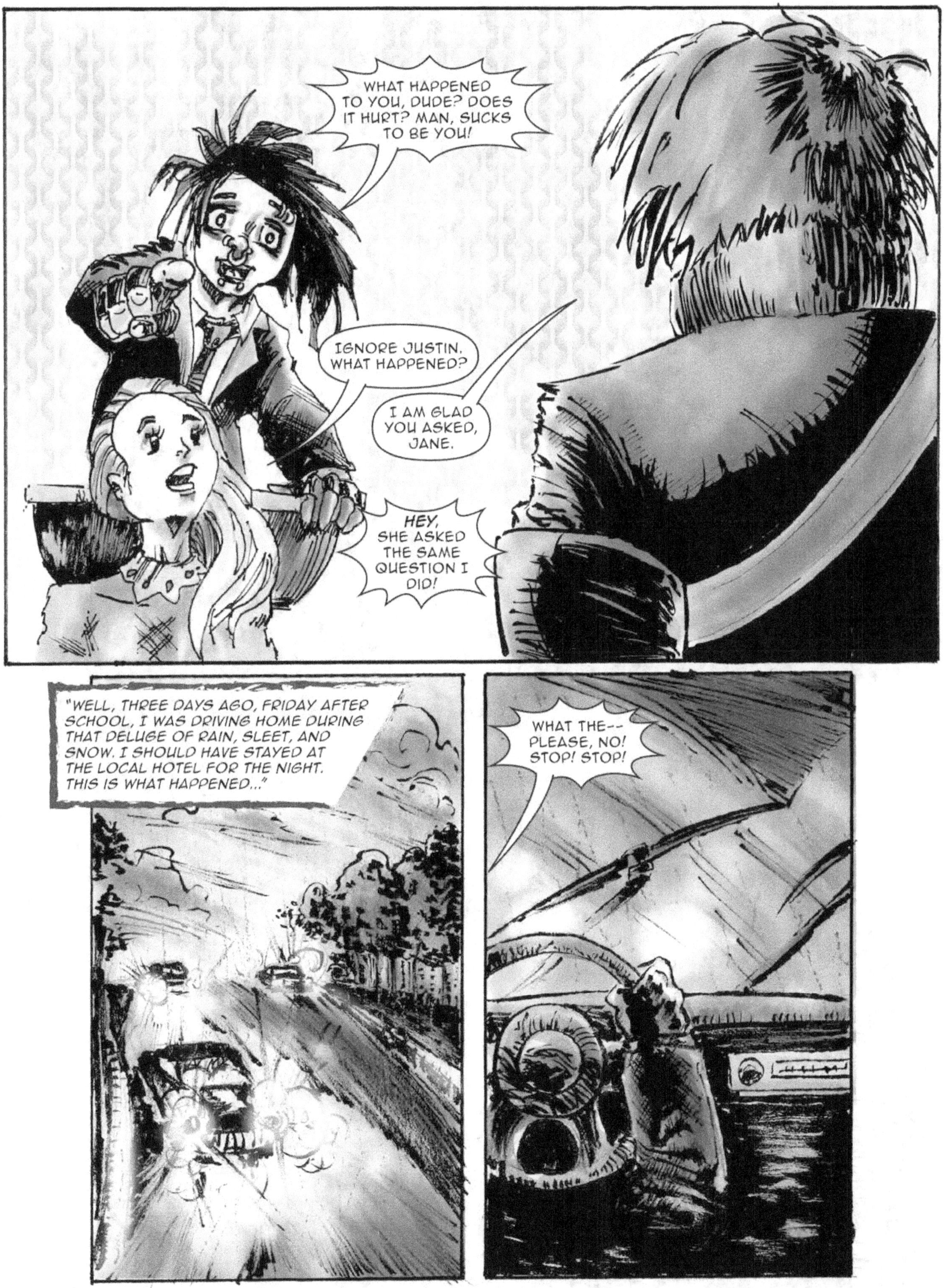

WHAT HAPPENED TO YOU, DUDE? DOES IT HURT? MAN, SUCKS TO BE YOU!

IGNORE JUSTIN. WHAT HAPPENED?

I AM GLAD YOU ASKED, JANE.

HEY, SHE ASKED THE SAME QUESTION I DID!

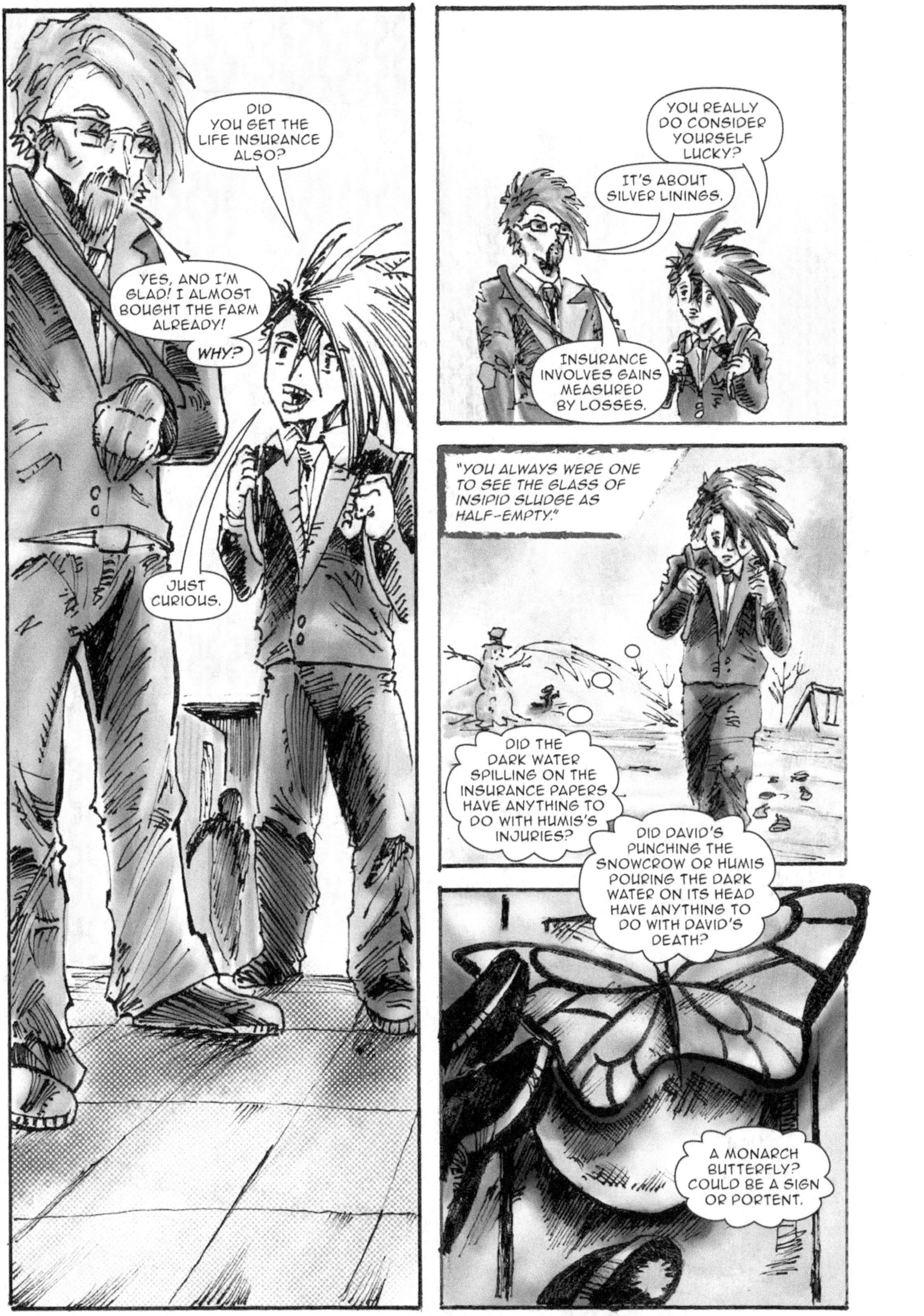

Dear Diary,

Jane told me today that the reason some people love or hate cilantro is because there is a genetic element to it. And then it got me thinking (not a good thing). What if food in general tastes different for person A and person B? Why else would one love pizza and the other despise it? To what extent is a person's taste palate influenced by culture or genetic makeup? And unless we can study an alternate universe in a test tube, we are stuck with a quasi-experiment with no real control and experimental groups. We are resigned to study twins reared apart or foster children reared together. And creating an alternate universe in a test tube would be even more difficult than finding a full suit of chain mail at a thrift shop (trust me, I have tried).

My dad had many of the same food sensibilities as myself (ugh, I hate talking about my dad in the past tense). He had a similar affinity for string cheese (and we both ate it like a celery stick as it took too long to peel like a banana). Whether I learned any of this from him or inherited these preferences from his genes is anybody's guess. And just like Dad's Levi jeans that Mom passed down to me, there are environmental factors to be considered as well (such as how the size of the pants is also affected by genetic makeup). Mom says I will fit into them soon enough. Maybe I will start a fashion trend by keeping one leg full length and the other one knee-length. I could call them "shants" or "ports." Why stop at jorts? One thing was for certain, my dad and I didn't share a "trail mix" gene. He always told me it was "dog food for humans." All I can say is if my dog Cat can eat human food it's only fair that I should be able to have some of hers! I am still trying to warm up to it. Maybe Cat is just more open minded than I am and I need to learn more about her canine culture. She is rather cosmopolitan.

Today in class I asked Professor Humis if he purchased life insurance in addition to the other supplemental plans that were part of

Pygmalion. He asked why I asked, and I told him I was just curious. It wasn't a lie per se, but it was not the whole truth either. Truth is, I "can't handle the truth" as was said in "A Few Good Men." But I didn't have a choice. The truth was right in front of me. At this point I feared for the Professor's life (I'm surprised he didn't notice my shaky hands or sweaty palms). And why shouldn't I be afraid? Every aspect of his insurance plan he purchased he ends up using sooner or later! Is it just a matter of time before he ends up using his life insurance as well? He insists he is lucky. But what if the insurance plan is causing his injuries?

As per Monday usual, I had therapy with Sylvia after school. We looked at the classes Jane and I would take next year when we started high school at the other side of town. Abnormal Psychology was on the list. Sylvia seemed excited about this, but I seized the moment to question and challenge what an oxymoron "Abnormal Psychology" was. I told Sylvia that any true scientist knows that all things happen for a reason (the crux of the scientific method). Every so-called "abnormal" behavior in that book is normal when you consider the context in which those behaviors occur. It would be more odd if they didn't occur, given the circumstances. Sylvia agreed with my general point, but she reminded me not to resort to the filibuster to avoid facing my emotions.

When I made my egress home I saw that there was a monarch butterfly sitting on the doorknob. And in February, no less! It triggered my memory of those Pygmalion insurance brochures and if there was any connection to the butterfly wings shown on the front cover. Does it have anything to do with the Butterfly Effect? Or the Pygmalion Effect? Self-fulfilling prophecy? Did the farm boy's skipping stone on the inside of the brochure represent the ripple effect? If the Professor hadn't asked for my stupid opinion, none of this would have happened. Kinda like how dad would be alive if he didn't walk under that ladder. Or how grandma would still be alive if mom hadn't made her get counseling. Is not this the Butterfly Effect? Bad things don't just happen when someone does something nefarious or with ill-intent. Even the most innocuous and benign little decisions can lead to someone's death. I don't blame mom for helping grandma see a therapist. But from a scientific standpoint, that tiny decision made the stars align in such a way as to ultimately lead to her demise. There are many a time travel movie or game where situations can be averted by changing the most minute little details. Or maybe I really was having delusions (and not the ones of grandeur).

For our supper tonight my mother made rice pudding for dessert. Rice of all things! It just triggered me to think about all the recent events once again. If Pygmalion Insurance was a corrupt company, would this further augment the dark-water properties into something even more sinister? Was this very rice pudding a perfect metaphor for such less-than-savory "just desserts"? Maybe the proof really was in the pudding.

They say "like father like son." Can the same be said for "like grandmother like grandson?" Sylvia seems to think it's all in my head. Even the most diehard and staunch skeptics that once proclaimed not believing in aliens or ghosts started believing when things started getting up close and personal. What is a "belief" anyway? Is it based on logic or wishful thinking (or in my case, un-wishful thinking)? And with the way things have been going, I was having a very up close and personal date with Lady Bad-Luck. Maybe real life really was like classic literature, where people, places, and things had meaning, symbolism, and allegory (much like "A Tale of Two Cities"). But any way you dice it, I did know something for certain—life was not like a box of chocolates but rather like a game of Othello. It requires patience. And the game is never over until it's really over. The tide can turn at any time. And just when you think you are in the lead, the entire board can "flip the script."

As a man of a scientific persuasion, I didn't just accept things as they were willy nilly. A good scientist knows when to reject the Null Hypothesis. And insofar that the Null Hypothesis represented my worst fears and everything I did not want to believe, I had to be at least 95% confident that I had enough evidence (or reassurances) to reject it with confidence.

All this anxiety and paranoia surrounding water science was making me very paranoid and hypervigilant in general, even in areas not related to water science. It's as if I was guarded, waiting for the next shoe to drop (hoping the next one wouldn't be a horse shoe). There are things I just don't feel ready to tell Jane or even mom (such as the dark thoughts and feelings I have been experiencing). Truth be told, there are things I haven't even told Sylvia. The last thing I needed was a 72 hour hold (I can't even handle being on hold on the phone for more than five minutes).

With all that said, Mr. Diary, there are times when I, you know, want to, well, it's hard to even say the word. Suffice it to say that you will know what it is by saying the first syllable of your name. But the more I think about it, I am just as afraid of death as I am about life. If only there was a 3rd option that didn't involve either one. I don't think I much like either of the choices I have been given. I suppose I could opt to be in a 20 year coma, but somehow that doesn't seem all that appealing either.

There are things in this world that leave me feeling ill at ease, such as the dog-eat-dog vigilantism of the food chain or the very laws of nature in and of itself. The mere fact that pain and death exist in the first place casts a net of Weltschmerz over my very being. I think 90% of the things people worry about are trivial and designed to distract us from the fact that we are all going to die and can't do anything about it. Even mate selection theory asserts that love is just an existential illusion, a chemical reaction to trick people into procreating. That sure takes the romance out of Casablanca.

CHAPTER 10.

THE CARROT

AND

STICK PRINCIPLE

Dear Diary,

I must admit, part of the reason I didn't take the bus was because I wasn't in the mood to sit next to Jane all the way home. Why did she take Sylvia's side like that? Speaking of busses, she sure threw me under one. Besides, I still needed to find a Valentine's Day gift for her (as much as I didn't really want to). This might be the first time I ever get a valentine from someone other than a teacher.

After I found a suitable pressie, I began walking home. When I got back to the school, I noticed Sylvia's yellow Prius was still there. I paused for a moment, staring at the school with a scowl on my face, thinking about her "kind and phony" offer to visit with her regarding Humiss death. How dare she profit off of tragedy like that? She may as well work for the evening news. Maybe Jane is in there with her and they are talking about me. Serves them right.

I paced in place to the tune of bruxism and fidgeting my hands around in my pockets. My hands bumped up against the same dime I stashed in there the day I got my foot caught in that wretched animal trap at Justin Banner's place. Sweet memories.

"Let's let the coin decide," I thought to myself. This didn't seem all that far-fetched. After all, it seemed as if fate was deciding everything else for me these days. I decided that if it landed on Heads, I would walk home as per my usual. If it landed on Tails (i.e. liberty, peace, and strength), I would take a chance and go visit Sylvia for what it was worth (if only to make Jane happy). At this point I was proving to be a real piece of work, and I didn't mean the Sistine Chapel. Maybe Sylvia could fix me Humpty Dumpty style.

I tossed the coin like a guy tossing a pizza. It twisted and twirled in the air, every little nuance and air current affecting it's spatial position. Lo and behold, my twisted fate decided to make it land on tails! Right about then I second-guessed flipping it in the first place.

Maybe I should have just walked home! Such shit luck! After a groan and/or grumble, I marched into Sylvia's office like a front line solder going into battle. If only I could have been one of the lucky ones to fall by the sword. I think I caught her off guard. She began rubbing the tears out of her eyes to hide the fact she was crying. Busted! I pretended that I didn't notice (although its possible that she pretended to not notice me pretending not to notice). I think that made sense. Either way, talk about Minnesota nice.

Sylvia may have felt embarrassed, but my trust for her increased after noticing that she was indeed a real human being after all. When you take "professionalism" too far you lose sight of yourself. There comes a point when all your responses start to sound robotic and scripted. I can spot a phony a mile away (1600 meters to those who want to eliminate imperial units). Small wonder they say A.I. will replace therapists in thirty years. Even the mental health guru Carl Rogers himself talked about the importance of "genuineness," "empathy," and "unconditional positive regard." When you lose the human element you lose altogether. But seeing her cry like that prompted me to begin an apology for calling her "fake" and "two-faced."

I stared at the floor and twisted my shoe around on the carpet as I murmured. "I'm like, you know, sorry and stuff, for what I said earlier."

Sylvia always said that apologies are easy. Anyone can do that. Turning the situation into a learning opportunity was her preferred manner of handling the situation (counselors and their conflict resolution and all that). She didn't just want the apology. She wanted an explanation too. I squirmed around not knowing what else to say. Sylvia just waited and smiled, allowing the awkward silence to linger (a favorite trick of counselors to get you to break your silence). But I was steadfast, and held my ground as if this was a verbal version of a staredown. I got her to break (well, not really, as she just prolonged the agony by telling me to "go ahead and think about it"). My gaze was averted from the floor and made eye contact. She was about to unearth yet another of my Achilles heels (with four by now I must be a horse). I explained to her how "murdering the messenger" was a defense mechanism of mine to add to the list. It was almost as if my pain and hurt were so raw that they would attack the most proximate target as if a dog biting a mailman. She reminded me that it was a form of emotional reasoning and not the stuff of "wise mind." I guess I spent too much time in "emotion mind" and "logic mind" and couldn't seem to find the happy medium. Perhaps I should re-read Goldilocks and the Three Bears. It sure beats Frosty the Snowman.

In the end, Sylvia lauded my insight into the matter and the fact that I gave her both an apology and an explanation. She went on to say that an apology without an explanation is the path of least resistance. And an explanation without an apology comes across as disingenuous and cold-hearted. But together the whole is greater than the sum of its parts. I guess I could buy that (along with Jane's present).

I sort of blurted out without thinking and asked if counselors have counselors of their own. She used the word "absolutely" and added that she sees one herself. I told her that maybe some counselors are human after all. Either that or they are replicants. Or maybe advanced robots with emotions, like Chappy.

Matters got a bit more serious as Sylvia's expression turned into a horizontal line (neither a smile or a frown). That meant she meant business. She stated that most people believe what they want to believe but that I had a tendency to believe what I didn't want to believe. A glutton for punishment," is how I think she put it. I explained to her how my worst fears were like a Null Hypothesis that I wanted to reject but couldn't until I had ample evidence and confidence.

Sylvia stood up, signaling to me that it was getting late and she wanted to return home. Despite that my visit was voluntary, can you believe she still gave me homework?

Our last dialogue was worthy of mention in and of itself. I still think therapists are phony robots, but maybe you are one of the good ones," I said. Sylvia smiled. "I wouldn't quit my job for the world."

"Yeah but just the other day you said yourself that most people would retire early if they had enough money and didn't have to work." Sylvia paused. "I'm not most people."

It turned out that I spent more time with Sylvia than my usual therapy sessions (on a Friday, no less). I just made it home in time to meet up with Jane at 5:30pm to play "Oriello." My mind was so distracted by everything that she ended up beating me for the very first time! I was a sore loser, and "tossed my cookies" towards her (not to be confused with projectile vomit). At least she wasn't a sore winner. Let's just hope she didn't let me win any of our previous games.

Jane pulled up the eerie photo from before, with David's supposed shadow near the fire hydrant. I asked her about it, expecting her to admit that she was feeling weirded out by the photo. Her answer wasn't quite what I expected. In fact, she said I was more dense than a black hole and it wasn't the ghost she was apprehensive about. When she said that "you seeing shadows is kind of scary" earlier she wasn't talking about the ghost or shadow. She was worried about me.

And Mr. Diary, you are probably wondering why I didn't mention what happened to Professor Humis. I know what happened to him from an objective standpoint. But it's as if my thoughts and feelings won't allow me to process it. I suppose Sylvia would call that denial. Either way, Humis's death was just another water-related death. My fears were only confirmed as Humis ended up using his life insurance that he had purchased from Pygmalion. At this point Professor Humis had used every single kind of insurance that he purchased: neck, arms, legs, and life itself. This wasn't even a Pyrrhic victory. He didn't use the insurance. The insurance used him.

I SEPARATED THE PLANT TYPES INTO CONTROL GROUPS AND EXPERIMENTAL GROUPS.

AREN'T YOU TOO COOL FOR WATER SCIENCE?

I'M A MYTHBUSTER

LOOKS LIKE WE ARE BOTH ROOTING FOR THE NULL HYPOTHESIS BUT FOR DIFFERENT REASONS.

I ALSO INTEND TO PUT AN END TO YOUR INSANITY FOR MY SAKE.

YOU ARE A "REVERSE TSUNDERE," STARTING OUT WARM AND ENDING UP COLD.

SOUNDS LIKE YOU SAID "SUNDEW," THE CARNIVOROUS PLANT.

I HAVE THREE TYPES OF PLANTS, EACH SEPARATED INTO THREE GROUPS.

POSITIVE WATER

NEGATIVE WATER

REGULAR WATER

ONE CONTROL GROUP WITH REGULAR WATER, ONE TREATMENT GROUP WITH POSITIVE WATER, AND THE THIRD GROUP WITH NEGATIVE WATER.

MY RESEARCH ISN'T SHOWING ANYTHING ALL THAT SIGNIFICANT, SAVE FOR A SIGNIFICANT WASTE OF TIME. EVEN THE PITCHER PLANTS ARE UNAFFECTED.

GOOD. WE CAN FINALLY PUT WATER SCIENCE TO BED

WELL, EXCEPT FOR THE VENUS FLY TRAPS, THAT IS.

WHAT DO YOU MEAN BY THAT?

IN THE SPIRIT OF VALENTINE'S DAY, CAN I ASK A QUESTION? IF "LOVE AT FIRST SIGHT" IS A THING, WHAT ABOUT "HATE AT FIRST SIGHT?"

"IF LOVE CAN EXIST AT FIRST SIGHT, I SUPPOSE HATE CAN AS WELL. WHY DO YOU ASK? IS THERE SOMEONE YOU ARE HATING ON?"

"NOT WITH PEOPLE PER SE. BUT SNOWMEN? THAT'S ANOTHER STORY."

YOU MAKE IT SOUND AS IF OUR ARCTIC FRENEMY WAS A HUMAN.

PEOPLE DON'T JUST FEAR WHAT THEY DON'T UNDERSTAND. THEY ALSO HATE WHAT THEY DON'T UNDERSTAND.

I GUESS HATE AND FEAR ARE TWO SIDES OF THE SAME COIN.

THAT COIN SURE ISN'T A DIME WITH OLIVE BRANCHES.

GRAB THAT SPADE AND BAG OF SOIL. DAD WANTED ME TO FILL ANOTHER POT FOR THE DWARF APPLE TREE. I ALSO HAVE TO TEND TO THOSE PITCHER PLANTS.

ACKNOWLEDGED.

THIS SPADE IS IN PRETTY TOUGH SHAPE. YOU TAKE OUT YOUR ANGST ON A LAMP POST?

THAT'S THE SPADE I USED TO KICK SOME SNOWCROW ASS LAST NIGHT.

TALK ABOUT CALLING A SPADE A SPADE!

SYLVIA WOULD SAY I'M JUST ENABLING YOUR SILLY NOTIONS.

IT'S BETTER TO BE SAFE THAN SORRY.

Dear Diary,

    People with diaries are literally writing a letter to a letter! Is this normal? Jane has resorted to comparing me to Grandma! The nerve! What hubris! That's tantamount to calling Othello Reversi. At least she filled me in on the entourage of snowcrows being built by Justin Banner and his minions. I still can't believe that just past midnight she literally went to bat for me and bashed a menagerie of snowcrows. She even burned their bodies and sent their gaseous souls up to the heavens. If that was an additional Valentine's Day gift it sure beats a box of chocolates (although I wouldn't turn down another Whitman's Sampler). There is nothing plain about this Jane.

    But if Jane or Justin think I am going to stay home forever they can think again. My plan when I come back is to prevent future tragedies from happening. An ounce of prevention really is worth a pound of cure. I wish they would convert that expression into metric. Then again, "28.3 grams of prevention is worth 0.454 kilograms of cure" doesn't quite have the same ring to it.

    In Othello terms, I am playing quiet, laying low, and allowing my canteen water to gain positive vibes! I will counter Justin Banner's loud tsunami with a quiet and subdued tesuji (one of the best moves in Othello). I guess you could say that I am planning an Othello-inspired "stoner trap" (in multiple senses of the phrase).

    But now onto Valentine's Day. Tis the season, after all. So how and why did a bleeding pulsating muscle (i.e. heart) ever become the quintessential symbol incarnate of amorous affection? There are fewer things more disgusting and/or repulsive, save for the sheep brains we dissected in biology class. Or that trail mix with the dried fruit. At least the brain has something to do with intellect by the end of the day. But what does the heart have to do with love? An organic pump that pushes blood around? There may sound alike on paper, but there is little similarity between a heart attack, heart burn, and a broken heart.

Perhaps an artificial heart could be the quintessential metaphor for superficial love. And a pacemaker could represent renewing one's vows.

And then we have Cupid's arrows. His "love-struck" victims are struck indeed, like the poor fellow in a crossbow accident. By any stretch, they should start calling "Valentine's Day" "Blood Pumping Muscle Day." At least it would be more accurate.

Jane gave me a cactus today as a Valentine's Day present, as a symbol of my resilience. She said to let it thrive and not to overwater it. Bless her (bloody pulsating) heart. What all this showed me was that behind Jane's tough outer shell is a candy center. She even promised to keep me up to date on my homework so I wouldn't fall behind.

Being away from the world of academia is the worst part about my little hiatus from the ivory tower. Sylvia said that mental disorders are best measured by how crippling they are in our various life roles and domains (like finances, relationships, and health). I have become rather accustomed to staying home and doing my homework. Why do I need to sit in a classroom to do that anyway? Tis' a shame Anomaly Academy doesn't have an online option like some modern universities. Of course, Sylvia would tell me that I am isolating. I call it solitude. But in my defense, I wonder if I even belong there with all those elitist class-holes.

I still can't get the late David Hinckley out of my mind (not to be confused with his penchant for tardiness and truancy). And I can say the same about the more recent death of Professor Humis. While I am at it, I might as well include dad and grandma's passings as well. It's a shame those who read this diary in a thousand years won't see the tears that are falling on these diary pages at this very moment (unless they somehow become fossilized for perpetuity). Maybe it's for the best. Who wants to see fossilized remnants of a maudlin dinosaur.

Mom, Jane, and Sylvia all know I am not exactly a happy camper these days. Although to be fair, are there any happy campers in a POW camp? I'm sorry, but I can't laugh myself out of this one. Only you, Dear Diary, knows the half of it. Even then, I'm not so sure words can even convey what I am feeling. After all, it takes 1000 words to describe one solitary picture.

Jane says I tend to "wear my heart on my sleeve" (an apt expression for today). I am working on getting better at "stuffing" or "compartmentalizing" my emotions (nobody knows the extent of my nervous disposition). My public self does not match my private one. And for now, I would like to keep it that way. Like a "functional drinker," I aim to be a "functional worry wart." And yet, Jane thinks I am as resilient as a cactus. I wish I could believe her. Maybe I should just hand it back and ask for a Weeping Willow instead.

Sylvia, mom, and Jane have been great, but how can they just live life like normal after what happened to Professor Humis and David? Or dad and grandma? Or any of the billions that have died in the past, present, or future for that matter? Death is a scary thing, isn't it? Am I crazy for admitting it? The reality is, when you deconstruct all your biases, illusions, delusions, and blind spots, Earth isn't all that different than a life and death reality show (Gantz, Hunger Games, or Running Man come to mind). It's even scarier when you realize that humans are technically animals and at the mercy of the same savage rules of nature. The "food chain" in and of itself makes me depressed. Predators and prey. Parasite and host. It's all so brutal.

Sylvia may call my condition apophenia and "terror management," but I prefer to think of myself as an existential detective. She says to not assume all coincidences are bad and look for the blessings in disguise. She said that ever since my dad and grandma died I have become a sort of puffed up porcupine. I could be poised for battle at a peace rally. It's a shame that all of us on Earth are resigned to walk through life on a "need to know" basis. If only we could break the fourth wall and get to the bottom of what this world is all about. Yup, I am talking about the meaning of life.

Death

The shine of metal that browns to rust
Or splendid flower that wilts to dust

The roar of river upon wall of stone
Or from womb to tomb when all become bone

When gale strikes hard and mountain peak erode
Or when acid spills and steel corrode

The fish upon sandy shore decay
Or the weavers cloth whose edges fray

Death will come as time goes past
But the fuse is short and it burns so fast

CHAPTER 12:

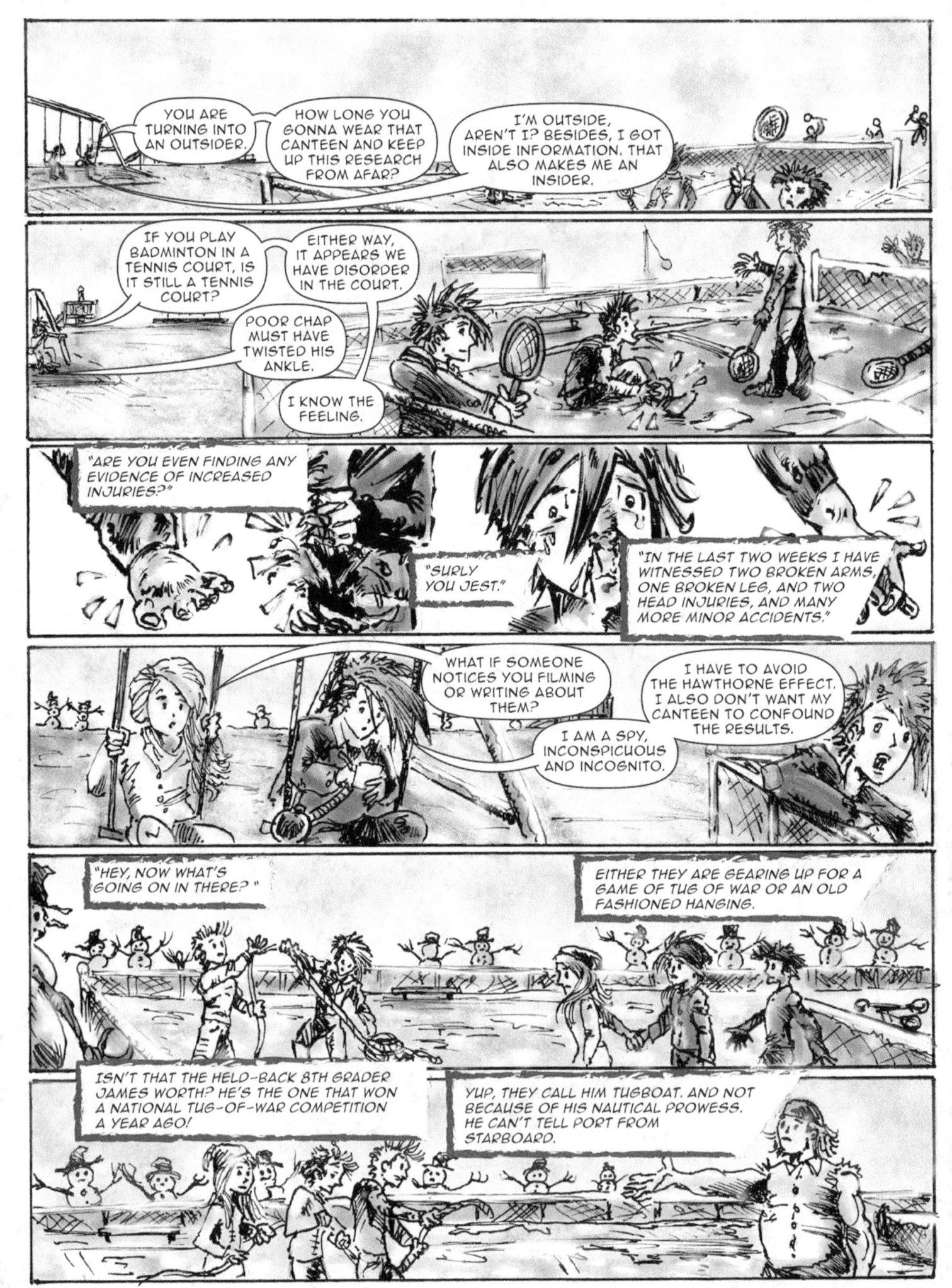

Fool's Gold April 1, 2016

Dear Diary,

It has been some time since I have written to you. Rest assured I had no intentions of giving you the silent treatment (although I am considering using these diary pages to write a treatment for a feature film). As for giving you the cold shoulder, that I can't rationalize. I guess with all the chaos lately I just wasn't in the mood for feathers and inkwells. But if I don't document these events soon, I may forget what transpired during these dark days. I'm just glad we are back on speaking terms (well, at least I am).

The tug-of-war incident came and went. Just like David Hinckley. And just like Professor Humis. One of the girls that lost multiple fingers, Sarah Dublin, died from sepsis some weeks ago. The moral of the horror story? One never knows when the fan is going to hit the shit (yup, I said that right, I'm referring to appliances being moved about by the likes of apparitions and poltergeists).

During the rest of March I continued to keep my daily planner in my pocket, and I kept track of accident data around the school. I played it cool and discreet, so nobody would be biased from the Hawthorne Effect. Yup, I quite literally and figuratively had a hidden agenda. And by the time the end of the month approached, I had witnessed four broken arms, three broken legs, and three head injuries, not to mention many other more minor accidents.

I even asked the school nurse if she kept statistics on school injuries. She said not really, although they did have some limited data from incident reports or the records they kept for purposes of "due diligence" and/or "ass-cover." Not only that, but they were in the process of an audit, keeping track of the safety risks of various forms of old-fashioned playground equipment they were thinking of phasing out. Although anecdotal, she did say that she noticed accidents were far higher these days than ever before. But what was the scientific mechanism or impetus behind such inexplicable events? Water science? The moon? Ocean tides? Supernatural forces? Plain old fashioned coincidence?

I couldn't help but notice that the city's Christmas decorations were still outside my window and adorning light poles around the neighborhood. Why stop at the 12 days of Christmas when you can do half a year? I can't say I am opposed to such an idea. I can almost hear my mother playing Elvis's "If Every Day Was like Christmas" from her vinyl collection.

It is now April, and the sun has finished off all the snow in Minneapolis after an insidious war of attrition between Sun vs. Snow. The sun won in the end. All the snowmen and snowcrows have since melted away into oblivion (even Justin's sleetipede). All except for our favorite cryptid that is, the original snowcrow by the red fire hydrant. He was the very last thing to melt in the entire school playground. How could that not be supernatural?

Jane had a different take. She said the snowman was very large. Not only that, but it resided in the cozy shade of the large oak and due to all this it's why it took longer to melt. Still, even the hill that kids played King of the Hill on had long dissipated by now, and that was much larger. And the piles of bull-dozed snow near the tennis courts had long since disappeared as well. It wasn't until today that the very last remnants of Frosty had been destroyed, leaving only two branches, pebbles, scarf, coal, and a rotten carrot on the concrete. And to think today was April Fools' Day!

I will never know what our good professor said or did to that water during those dark days. Maybe it's best we never know. I hoped that after this ordeal I would have at least gained a level like in an RPG (like moving from an apprentice to a mage). In my case, I seemed to have evolved from a whipper-snapper into a whipping-boy. And to be honest, I am not sure which was better. Maybe it's best to call it a lateral move.

What about Jeremy Pegg? He is still working with Sylvia through his shame and guilt for feeling responsible for killing David. But I have to admit, I did catch him laughing in the locker room a few times and when he made eye contact with Sylvia he reprised his grimace and frown (giving credence to the theory that he has since gotten over his troubles and is malingering just to keep seeing Sylvia).

So have I become less superstitious since these events? According to Sylvia, I have made "leaps and bounds" (whatever that means). Then again, she can be a bit Pollyanna and it's hard to say how many of her compliments are genuine. But at least I am back at school, which says something (although the absences of David, Sarah, and Professor Humis are glaring). I am working on accepting the fact that life is just one big shit storm with no real rhyme or reason. I am calling this newfound mindset "cynical optimism." Still, I find it best to not wander under ladders willy-nilly. Good Othello players know that a little quiet caution and patience will win the game.

But I better put my pen down. They are predicting an April blizzard, and they are starting to list the school closings...

Extras

CHARACTER BIO DESCRIPTIONS

Teddy Jales: Teddy is a curious 14-year-old in the 8th grade. They say it was curiosity that killed the cat. But you wouldn't want to put that prospect past Teddy either (not to mention Teddy's Corgi is named Cat). Teddy is indecisive by nature and will often jump back and forth between positions or perspectives. Mind you, Teddy is also very troubled when it comes to matters of the mind (or mind over matter for that matter).

Jane Avalon: Jane is a no-nonsense and responsible 14-year-old in the 8th grade. The "absolute value" of Teddy's curiosity is matched in full by Jane's sarcasm and eye roll velocity. She is Teddy's faithful sidekick (or is it the other way around?) Either way, there are times when Jane wouldn't mind giving Teddy a good "kick in the side." Jane and Teddy are both raised by single parents, in Jane's case it's her father.

David Hinckley: Teddy's feisty classmate. Unlike Jane, David is a non-sense and irresponsible sort. Some might even liken him to a bully (although if you asked him he would say that only bullies would call him a bully). He is 14 and is in 8th grade and likes to play King of the Hill with the younger students. Many have hypothesized that it's because he likes to have an unfair size advantage. Or maybe it's because he has his own brand of "prep school" and aims to prep the younger students for the tough years ahead. He attends the same science class as Jane and Teddy taught by Professor Travis Humis.

Professor Travis Humis: Teddy's 45-year-old and socially awkward science teacher at Anomaly Academy. He is fond of the fact that he Is teaching the very first college level course on supernatural physics in the country (to the chagrin of no-nonsense scientists that would never entertain such fanciful notions). Humble to a fault, he doesn't mind being called Travis but the school administration insists the students call him "Professor." He was never married and has no children. He has the largest collection of sedimentary rocks in the tristate area.

Karen Jales: Teddy's thirty-five-year-old mother. She works full time as a bank teller. She bears the brunt of Teddy's inquisitive nature (for good or ill). Karen and Teddy have a common bond over the fact that Derek Jales (Karen's husband and Teddy's father) passed away some years ago. While the subject has become somewhat of an elephant in the room, we all know that you can't just sweep an elephant under a rug willy-nilly. And despite any remnants of Midwest stoicism that may or may not be present in either person, their voluminous tears flow freely and often.

Derek Jales: Teddy's 45-year-old father and Karen's husband. He reprised his role as a research psychologist in Minneapolis after a short stint as a Social Psychology Professor. He loathed the "publish or perish" mindset of mainstream academia so he left the university system as soon as he entered it. Not being one to be told what to do, he enjoyed a carte blanche and laissez-faire control over his very own lab. He taught Teddy that "non-significant" studies are every bit as important as the ones that show significant results (as it's important to know what treatments don't work in addition to the ones that do work).

Lydia Jales: Teddy's 75-year-old kind but troubled grandmother. She is superstitious to a fault and will partake in any ritual she can to "dispel" any bad outcome from coming to fruition (regardless of how many are watching her). She enjoyed (if that's the right term for the rest of us) over 30 years of work as a certified tax preparer. One of her favorite things to do just after the holidays was to donate her time to prepare taxes for free for those with limited incomes. They say death and taxes are the only certainties in life. And suffice to say Lydia proved the notion on both counts.

Justin Banner: Teddy's fellow and mysterious 15-year-old classmate and "frenemy" (held back one year). He has all the appearances of a goth teen, but don't let appearances fool you. He is no poser. In fact, his intellectual musings on the "futility of mortality" matched his dressage like hand and glove (a tattooed hand in a black leather glove to be more exact). His pessimism makes almost anyone feel ill at ease in his wake (not to be confused with the funeral variety).

Sylvia Koch: Teddy's 28-year-old and recently married school counselor. Teddy's mother made the decision that Teddy needed to talk to Sylvia to process the passing of his dad, Derek (Karen also hoped that Teddy would come home and share some of Sylvia's "sage wisdom" with her over dinner to help her heal as well). It was well-known (among students) that many would pretend to have problems just to have an excuse to see her.

Jeremy Pegg: An 8th grader of Anomaly Academy and a longtime friend of Teddy. As a square peg in a round hole, he often finds himself at the wrong place at the wrong time. When the school counselor (Sylvia Koch) asked him what he wanted to be when he grew up, he stated that his sole mission in life was to topple David Hinckley at a game of King of the Hill. In a perfect world, confidence and competence should match. However, the fact that Jeremy saw himself more as a Court Jester than a King certainly didn't help matters much.

James Worth (AKA Tugboat): 15 year old held-back 8th grader (and Tug of War aficionado). While David Hinckley would beat James at King of the Hill every time, the same could be said about James's victories over David at Tug of War. James has won several regional championships in the "sport." It was never verified if true, but James claimed that he won a game of Tug of War with him on one end and three upper classmen on the other.

Alissa Weimarck: Eighth grader and 14 year old long-time friend of Jane Avalon (as evidenced by their "friendship promise rings" they promised they would never take off as long as they remained friends). While Jane had never been the sports type, there wasn't a single track and field event that Alissa didn't excel at. What drew Alissa and Jane together was their mutual love of horticulture, greenhouses, and gardening. They even started an online blog together called "Seeds and Weeds."

TEDDY

Jane

DAVID

Professor Humis

TEDDY

Character Page

Character Page 2

Page 15

mom→

tedy→

Page 16

People in street side walk

Page 11   Issue 3

Exageration
Haunting panel (1)
2 walking st..11

warm light windows
HOME!!

HOME IS WHERE THE HEART IS!

Snowcrow: The Graphic Novel by Blake Alb

General notes:

Cover Art: Something that "screams" Snowcrow (immediately brings to mind novella version)

Main character clothing notes: Very "wintery" all around

Teddy: In general, in indoor settings such as at home, he wears a beige cable-knit sweater (as per the novella). Outdoors, he tends to wear a black peacoat over his clothes. In school, though, he has the "Anomaly Academy" school uniform (v-neck navy blue sweater with crest-like DNA strand symbol embroidered on it). Teddy is 14 and in eighth grade. For his appearance, I am thinking an anime/manga look, maybe something like Becky Cloonan would sketch.

Jane: If she is indoors, she can have a fleece jacket, hoodie, or flannel. When outside, she can have a red peacoat. She has the same school uniform as Teddy when indoors (Anomaly Academy V-neck sweater, DNA strand embroidered on it). Jane is also 14 and in eighth grade. Manga appearance.

Professor Travis Humis: Formal suit or shirt and tie. He is 45. He can look like your depiction of a "stereotypical professor" (have fun with the caricature). Manga appearance. His beard in the preliminary sketches that John did looked awesome.

David Hinckley: Leather jacket and jeans. He is 13 and is in 7th grade. He still likes to play King of the Hill with the 5th and 6th graders. He also attends the same science class as Jane and Teddy, taught by Professor Travis Humis. He has a manga appearance. He likes to wear his leather jacket over his school uniform.

Notes about Anomaly K-8 Academy: This is a private K-8 school, very expensive, for kids who show academic potential (some kids get scholarships to help pay for it). Elementary and middle school are combined in the same building. There is a playground outside (used mainly by the kids in Kindergarten through 6th grade during their noon-hour recess). However, the middle schoolers (7th and 8th graders) also get lunch hour off, and they can either use it as a study hall or to go outside, mingle, and relax around the playground. The older elementary age kids (5th or 6th graders) might partake in more rough and tumble sport, such as King of the Hill, kill the carrier, or snowball fights. Middle schoolers in 7th or 8th grade sometimes play basketball or tennis in the courts.

Snowcrow: The Graphic Novel by Blake Alb

Issue 1

Chapter 1: When Hell Freezes Over!!

January 28, 2016

Panel 1 (full page, start of chapter): For this chapter pic, one idea is to show the large snowman (with a mysterious dent in its midsection, where a cell phone is sitting). Perhaps we could have an ambulance in the background, depicting emergency staff carrying a stretcher! Perhaps there could be a border around the scene, showing a sort of "frozen fire" effect to call attention to the name of the chapter.

Panel 2: Teddy is sitting on the swing next to Jane. They are casually chatting as they watch the other kids playing on the nearby playground equipment (slide, jungle gym, Merry Go Round, etc.). Heavy snow is falling, casting very wintery vibes. Teddy is wearing a black pea-coat and Jane a red one over their school uniforms. Narration bubble text at top of panel: Noon break at Anomaly Academy K-8 School, Minneapolis, MN, January 28, 2016

Panel 3: Same playground, different view of them on swings (you can play around with creative camera angles). Kids are having a snowball fight nearby. School (Anomaly Academy) can be seen in the background as well. There is a "slippery when wet" pylon near the slide.

Panel 4: Fifth and sixth graders can be seen playing King of the Hill near the swingset, and in front of an ominous and salient fire hydrant. Several kids can be seen toppling down like bowling pins as burly sixth grader David Hinckley maintains his position at the top. Remember, David is a 13-year-old 7th grader, and is a little bit larger than the other 5th and 6th graders he is fighting against. Panel 5: Only Teddy and Jane's faces can be seen. They are looking/chatting at each other. Jane can be seen pointing towards the hill towards David with her finger or thumb.

Panel 6: David is standing proudly at the top of the hill, kids falling down the slopes.

Panel 7: Another shot of the kids playing King of the Hill, David is being even more aggressive than usual. A couple of kids can be seen writhing in pain near the foot of the hill. Note: No dialogue in this panel, save for maybe some groans and grunts!

Panel 8: At the top of the hill stand two kids in particular, David Hinckley and a 6th grader, Jeremy Pegg. There are three kids standing at the bottom of the hill watching the battle ensue. Jane and Teddy are in the distance, casually sitting on their swings. Same weather, feel free to use light snow instead of heavy if you wish, use your discretion :)

Panel 9: Similar setting as before, different angle maybe, Teddy and Jane look more concerned. The bystanders look slack-jawed at the impending drama, some with their hands on their mouths. Jeremy has his pockets hanging out of his jeans, proving he does not have the phone.

Panel 10: Jeremy is standing, the whites of his pockets hanging out.

Panel 11: Jeremy scrapes his foot against the ground, as if a bull preparing to charge. David is seen putting his hands out, as if trying to change Jeremy's mind.

Panel 12: Jeremy is seen pushing David over the edge, and David loses his balance!

Panel 13: David is shown falling by the large snowman, horizontal on the ground. Bystanders are laughing at him!! How dare they!

Panel 14: Bystanders are still laughing, and David is standing up, brushing snow off his pants.

Panel 15: Teddy and Jane are looking at each other from their stationery swings, quite enthralled by the ensuing drama. Try to use the open space on the right of the panel for some of the dialogue if possible.

Panel 16: David punches a hole in the midsection of the snowman. Puffs of snow surround the punch area.

Panel 17: David is turned around from the snowman, now facing Jeremy (Jeremy is not in the frame, however).

Panel 18: Now Jeremy can be seen on top of the hill, facing David (David is not in the panel). Jeremy is too fearful to be proud of his newfound alpha position on the hill.

Panel 19: Jeremy is shown stepping away as if a posh waiter at an upscale restaurant. David flounders past, losing gravity and gaining momentum!

Panel 20: David is seen losing his balance, arms flailing. Ominous fire hydrant is shown, again calling attention to itself via creative camera angles and juxtaposition of the artwork.

Panel 21: David is lying there, motionless, as onlookers appear agasp.

Panel 22: Onlookers are coming in for a closer look. Two of David's tough-looking friends are leaning down towards him, as if staring at the corpse of an alien. Jeremy Pegg is present, looking scared, guilty, and ashamed.

Panel 23: A river of blood can be seen running from David's head injury due to hitting the fire hydrant. Bystanders are standing around agasp, some with hands on their mouths. There is no fog coming out of David's mouth, indicating no breathing. Jeremy Pegg is there, hand over mouth, mortified by what he has contributed to. Note: Maybe a "whack" sound effect is coming from the hydrant.

Panel 24: Teddy and Jane dash away from their swings, with horrified expressions.

Panel 25: Teddy and Jane join the crowd of onlookers, tired from running, and share their shock and surprise. Teddy is holding his phone, ready to dial.

Panel 26: Only Teddy and Jane are visible in this panel. Teddy is holding the cell phone to his ear, just after dialing 911. Jane is starting to make a mad dash to fetch Mary Thompson, the recess monitor.

Panel 27: Recess monitor steps onto the scene (she is about 47 years old). She has large glasses and a long brown trench coat. She is also wearing a large hat with ear lappers. She appears shocked and panicked. Jane is with her, out of breath from running. Only Mary, Jane, and Teddy can be seen in the panel, as they hover over David.

Panel 28: Worried onlookers stare while Mary administers CPR. Jeremy Pegg is also present, looking almost sick to his stomach.

Panel 29: One more dramatic panel showing CPR, this time revealing a worried, tired, and sweaty look on Mary's face, indicating that she has been trying for quite some time. Some additional worried faces might be seen behind her (including Jeremy Pegg, feeling guilty for his part in the accident).

Panel 30: Ambulance shows up, responders coming to the scene. Mary is standing to the side. A thirty-something female responder is holding a medical case. Jeremy Pegg is standing next to the female, almost hindering her work.

Panel 31: The female and another twenty-something male first responder are placing David on a stretcher. Jeremy is watching in disbelief.

Panel 32: The snowman is shown, a gaping hole in its abdomen. David's missing cell phone is sitting in the hole!! The snowman's head is askew, looking at the fire hydrant where David hit his head. Teddy and Jane are looking at the hole and the phone.

Panel 33: Teddy is sitting in his bedroom, wearing his normal "indoor" outfit (beige cable-knit sweater). His room is fairly messy, with clothes strewn about. He is sitting on his bed, looking towards the window wistfully, with a thought bubble above his head.

Panel 34: He walks towards his writing desk.

Panel 35: Teddy is sitting at his writing desk, tapping his chin with his pencil.

Panel 36: Teddy has his pencil poised over the page.

Teddy's Diary

Chapter 2: "Icy Scrutiny" and "Leisure Seizures"
December 14, 2015 (about a month ago)

Panel 1 (full page, start of chapter 2): Teddy and Jane are wearing peacoats and making snow angels in the snow outside Teddy's home. It's a more light-hearted and happy moment. Maybe exaggerate the "Christmas vibe" in this full-page illustration (like a Terry Redlin or Norman Rockwell painting). Snowfall, nostalgia, old-fashioned vibes, etc.

Panel 2: Teddy (in cable knit sweater) is in his home, sitting on his knees on the sofa, staring at the snow out the window. His Corgi dog "Cat" is standing on the armrest, also staring out the window with Teddy. There is a Christmas tree visible in the panel also along with various ornaments and X-mas vibes. Winter Wonderland playing on vinyl throughout the house, indicating festive Christmas music, maybe some music notes indicating audio.

Panel 3: Teddy is now sitting properly on the couch, aiming the remote at the TV, and turning it on to see the school closings. The Corgi (named Cat) is sitting near Teddy.

Panel 4: Most of the panel is the TV screen, showing school closings. The text bar at the bottom of the screen states: Hennepin and Anthony middle schools, no school. Sanford and Sullivan middle schools, buses running two hours late…

Panel 5: Teddy is petting the dog as they both watch the TV in earnest anticipation.

Panel 6: Teddy is now staring at his dog and speaks to her, as if she can understand.

Panel 7: Similar to before, but different "camera angle." Teddy is looking at the fireplace, priming a line of discussion. Teddy is still talking to Cat without looking at her, and Cat appears to almost understand.

Panel 8: Teddy's mom (Karen Jales) enters the room with a large feather duster in her hand and begins dusting the television.

Panel 9: Karen is holding a picture of her deceased husband (Teddy's dad), Derek Jales, as Teddy clicks off the TV.

Panel 10: Frosty the Snowman is playing in the background (as shown by music notes). The record skips on the same spot, repeating the line: "before I melt away, before I melt away, before I melt away." Karen is walking towards wherever the record player is located (it may be outside the panel). Teddy looks concerned.

Panel 11: A creepy close-up shot of someone knocking (one time) using the very ominous old-fashioned lion door knocker on the front door. The medallion takes up most of the panel. There is a sound effect of the knock.

Panel 12: Teddy and Karen are looking at each other incredulously.

Panel 13: Teddy walks towards the door to answer it.

Panel 14: Teddy is standing on the porch (wearing a black peacoat), and Jane can be seen in the snow above the lawn. Jane is making a snow angel, but Teddy thinks she may be having a seizure! Jane is wearing a red peacoat.

Panel 15: Jane pauses her arm motions.

Panel 16: The wider shot depicts neighboring houses, calling attention to the socially awkward moment of Jane making a fool of herself. There are a couple of people walking along the sidewalk who can't help but notice.

Panel 17: They are both flailing about, two adjacent snow angels. Snow is being blown about, like debris being whittled off a statue.

Panel 18: Teddy and Jane are standing up, admiring their handwork, two nice snow angels adjacent to each other.

Panel 19: The snow angels are still visible in the panel, but Jane and Teddy are looking at each other, more seriously than before; gone are their jovial countenances.

Panel 20: Jane has an empathetic/caring look on her face as she faces Teddy.

Panel 21: A side-by-side shot of a snow angel and a snowman, sort of comparing the two. Teddy and Jane's thought bubbles are shown (off camera) as if they are talking in the distance.

Panel 22: Teddy writing diligently, tongue out, licking his lips deep in thought.

Panel 23: Teddy writing, different angle, more words on the page.

Panel 24: Teddy with bloodshot eyes.

Panel 25: Teddy asleep on his desk, pencil in hand. Teddy's Diary --

Issue 2
Notes for John Davies: As before, feel free to add additional non-dialogue action shots as you see fit to fill to 22 pages etc.

Chapter 3: Where There is Smoke, There are Mirrors
December 18, 2015

Panel 1 (full page, start of chapter 3): There are two large jars sitting on a shelf. Sitting next to the jar on the left is a framed picture depicting a white parrot (symbol of positivity). Next to the jar on the right is a statue of a gargoyle. Between the two jars is a statue of a snowman with a flat expression. There are grains of rice in each jar. The jar on the left has a label it that says "Good vibes," and the jar on the right has a label that says "Bad vibes."

The jar on the right contains rice that is nasty, fermented, rotten, etc. The rice on the left looks healthy and intact.
Panel 2: wide shot of classroom, maybe 10 students or so. Professor Travis Humis is wearing a suit and tie. He is 45 years old. He is standing at a lectern like a college Professor. There is an image of the book cover for "The Hidden Messages of Water" by Masaru Emoto shown on the classroom screen (computer, of course, not old old-fashioned projector). School yard bully David Hinckley is sitting in the back row, leather jacket worn over his school uniform. Feel free to add a subtle element of racial diversity with the students (nothing too drastic, we want to avoid making it look "forced" or "political").
Panel 3: David, blurting out without raising his hand. Professor Humis can also be seen in the shot, other kids are staring back at him, awkwardly. Teddy and Jane are visible as well, in the very front row.
Panel 4: Humis is looking mockingly at David. Teddy whispers to Jane.
Panel 5: showing classroom and all four main characters, Professor Humis, Jane, Teddy, and David Hinckley):
Panel 6: Teddy's desk is shown up close, with the scrape and scratch of students etching band names (Quiet Riot, ACDC, Nirvana, Green Day, and Enya).
Panel 7: Classroom, different "camera angle." He is holding a very unique textbook called "Paranormal Science." It says "Teacher Edition" on the front.
Panel 8: Humis continues, unabashed.
Panel 9: Humis pulls out two jars from inside the podium and holds them up.
Panel 10: Humis sets the two jars on his desk near the podium.
Panel 11: Class appears attentive.
Panel 12: Class breaks out in peals of laughter.
Panel 13: Class shot, different "camera angle." Teddy and Jane are whispering to each other.
Panel 14: Humis is walking around the classroom, away from the podium, on one side of the room. He is holding the book "The Hidden Messages of Water" by Masaru Emoto.
Panel 15: Humis is mingling around the room, from different camera angles.
Panel 16: Humis, staring out the door into the empty hallway, continues his lecture with his back turned to the students.
Panel 17: Humis turns away from the door and faces the class. Teddy's Diary

Chapter 4: Bird Nuggets (of Wisdom)
Christmas Morning, December 25, 2015

Panel 1 (full page, start of chapter 4): A very creepy snowman is shown, the bottom (largest) part of his body consisting of a large Magic Eight Ball (with the message "It is certain" written in the window). The snowman appears ragged and disheveled, like a scarecrow. The school playground suddenly looks like a graveyard, tombstones littered about, intermingled around the playground equipment. I think you can have lots of fun with this one. Try to make it more scary than funny, if that makes sense! Maybe since it's Christmas, add some border art to indicate a Christmas vibe (string of lights, garland, etc.).
Panel 2: The kitchen of the Jales home. Traditional kitchen, no island counter, just a table in the center of the room. It's a modest home, not elitist or superfluous. Fridge, microwave, toaster, sink, perimeter counter, etc. Elvis' "Blue Christmas" is playing on the record player. Karen Jales (Teddy's mother, 43 years old) is making waffles. The Corgi dog "Cat" by her side. Teddy looks tired and can be seen in the doorway. Karen is wearing an apron over a blouse. Teddy is wearing either his typical cable-knit sweater (you can make it a Fair Isle sweater if you think it should look more Christmas). There are various Christmas decorations around the kitchen.
Panel 3: Karen is resting her chin on her palms, her elbows on the table. She has a concerned look.
Panel 4: Teddy and Karen are sitting on opposite sides of the table. There is a big stack of waffles on a plate in the center of the table. They both have food on their plates, as they have already served themselves. There is some Christmas décor on the table as well.
Panel 5: Close-up of Karen, looking towards the "camera" incredulously (as if looking at Teddy inquisitively).
Panel 6: An Othello board covered with cookies, some with the chocolate side on top, and others with the vanilla side on top.
Panel 7: Karen and Teddy in conversation, different camera angle, maybe. Karen is pouring maple syrup on her waffles.
Panel 8: They are eating their food together.
Panel 9: Teddy is reading the syrup bottle (close-up shot). It says 1% real maple syrup.
Panel 10: Karen's face is the main part of the panel, smiling.
Panel 11: Teddy and Karen are leaning back in their chairs, a bit tired from their food.
Panel 12: different expressions, different camera angles, etc.
Panel 13: Teddy's worried face is shown.
Panel 14: Karen adopts a much more caring demeanor and expression. Teddy dons a worried look of consternation.
Panel 15: Karen is now sitting next to Teddy on the sofa, arm around his shoulders. The living room looks similar to before.
Panel 16: Close-up of Karen's sad face as she opens up about the family deaths.
Panel 17: Flashback scene of Teddy's dad, Derek, walking under a large window-washer's ladder in Keystone, South Dakota. Karen and Lydia Jales are also with him (but not walking under the ladder).
Panel 18: Flashback of Grandma Lydia Jales holed up in her own living room (in her own house) peering out the window in a paranoid fashion, with a glazed 1000-yard stare.
Panel 19: Flashback of Lydia Jales in the therapist's office. She is opening up an umbrella indoors in the presence of the male therapist, to face her fears and prove once and for all that nothing weird will happen.
Panel 20: Shot of the building where Lydia receives therapy. The building is on a hill, and there are many steps leading up to the main entrance. Lydia Jales is shown slipping on icy concrete (or stone) steps, the top-most step, falling backwards (about to break her neck).
Panel 21: Close-up of Teddy's worried face.
Panel 22: a picture of a "normal bell curve" from statistics.
Panel 23: This shot can show two framed photos of Derek (Teddy's dad) and Lydia (Teddy's grandma) shortly before they died.
Panel 24: Living room. Karen and Teddy are on the couch, a different camera angle than usual to mix it up a bit.
Panel 25: Living room. Karen looks excited.
Panel 26: Teddy opens up a new Othello board game (a fancy wooden version)
Panel 27: Teddy opens up a large plastic canister of trail mix.
Panel 28: Teddy opens up a Magic Eight Ball toy (new in box, ball is visible in window packaging)!
Panel 29: Teddy is holding the Magic Eight Ball out of the box and starts shaking it.
Panel 30: Close-up shot of Magic Eight Ball. It says, "It is certain."
Panel 31: Teddy shakes it again.
Panel 32: Teddy looks through the window of the Eight Ball, looking much more concerned than before.
Panel 33: Teddy is shaking it for dear life, and Karen looks very worried.
Panel 34: Teddy is staring down the Eight Ball as if he were having a staredown with a cobra.
Panel 35: Karen shakes the ball. Teddy is peering over her shoulder nervously, face flushed.

Panel 36: Teddy looks resigned and withdrawn, staring blankly at the floor. Karen is next to him, holding the eight ball on her lap.
Panel 37: Karen is walking to the kitchen, and Teddy stays behind. Teddy's Diary Examples of Teddy's "Accent Fonts"

Issue 3

Chapter 5: Don't Let it Snow, Don't Let it Snow, Don't Let it Snow....
Christmas afternoon, December 25, 2015

Panel 1 (full page, start of chapter 5): Maybe a scary depiction of sleetipede to introduce the chapter, like a scene from Teddy's nightmares.
Panel 2: Teddy is sitting on the edge of his bed, too worried to partake in X-mas festivities. His bedroom includes such things as: book bookshelf of all sorts of books, manga, graphic novels, etc. The Magic Eight Ball and a can of trail mix are on the desk by his computer. There is a window, and the Christmas lights outside the house are imbuing a warm glow to the bedroom. There is a large clock on the wall, indicating 2:00 PM. Typical things like a closet, clothes strewn on the floor, etc. There is also a large box of "Whitman's Sampler" on the bed. He is wearing the same cable knit sweater from the morning.
Panel 3: Teddy is facing the window, a 12-foot MASSIVE snowman in the neighbor's yard (the home of fellow 8th grade student and goth kid Justin Banner). The "snowman" is essentially a "snow-centipede" standing vertically. It is composed of four segments (instead of the usual 3 for typical snowmen). Each of the four "balls" is about 3 feet in diameter. There are long sticks for insect legs and two large novelty candy cane yard ornaments for antennae (which are large enough to actually use as a real cane to walk with). Panel 4: Teddy is shown using his binoculars (the border of the panel can be made to look like a view from binoculars). You can more clearly see the 12-foot ominous snow-centipede in Justin Banner's yard. There is also a "Keep Off Property" and "Beware of Dog" sign. There is also a gargoyle statue on each side of the door, sitting on the porch of the house.
Panel 5: Teddy is wearing his binoculars around his neck.
Panel 6: Teddy is putting on his coat and scarf from the closet.
Panel 7: Teddy is walking downstairs, looking sombre. He is also wearing a scarf.
Panel 8: Karen is sitting on the sofa in the living room, reading a magazine. Christmas music is playing in the house.
Panel 9: Teddy is standing in the doorway, dressed for winter. He is also wearing fingerless gloves and a stocking cap (beanie). Panel 10: A man is seen falling down in front of an oncoming truck and gets hit. Use hyperbole to play up the fear, as it's sort of a window in Teddy's mind and his penchant for "catastrophizing."
Panel 11: A woman is shown in a hospital room, recovering from (apparently) being poisoned and almost dying. Feel free to use hyperbole to play up the fear, as it's sort of a window in Teddy's mind.
Panel 12: A grown woman gives a younger girl a swirly in a toilet.
Panel 13: A nice pic of a water molecule, all nice and innocent, supposedly. Maybe draw an owl nearby as well, saying "hoo." Panel 14: Neighborhood shot, sidewalks, houses, etc. Teddy is walking, deep in introspection. Light snow is falling. Christmas ornaments and decorations abound. There are also a handful of people milling about. There are Christmas decorations around, like candles or little X-mas trees on the light poles.
Panel 15: Teddy is walking, hands in pockets, thinking to himself.
Panel 16: Teddy slaps himself in the face quite hard.
Panel 17: Teddy looking pensive, imitating a caricature of a Zen Buddhist deep in thought.
Panel 18: Random images of a tapir, a toilet paper tube, and a shoe horn.
Panel 19: An image of a 1852 calendar, outlet cover, and a vomit stain from 1971.
Panel 20: Creepy snowman (i.e., snowcrow) holding a bleeding three-footed rabbit, and wearing a lucky rabbit's foot around his neck.
Panel 21: Image of Teddy fending off a snowcrow's barrage of snowballs, using an umbrella as if it were a shield.
Panel 22: Cover of book "The Hidden Messages in Water" by Masaru Emoto.
Panel 23: Teddy reaches into his pocket.
Panel 24: A close shot of Teddy's hand looking at a dime (tail side, with the torch, olive branch, and oak branch).
Panel 25: Teddy resumes his leisurely jaunt as he places the dime into one of the pockets of his peacoat. He looks pensive and contemplative.
Panel 26: Teddy stops in his tracks, facing the massive 12-foot four-piece ominous snow-centipede in Justin Banner's yard. There is a "Keep Off Property" and "Beware of Dog" sign. There are two gargoyle statues, one on each side of the door, sitting on the porch of the house.
Panel 27: The two signs and porch gargoyles take center stage in this panel.
Panel 28: Teddy takes a little baby step onto the property, just to feel rebellious.
Panel 29: Teddy takes a step and steps right into an animal trap (like a fox trap)! He is wailing in pain. It's pretty severe, the trap breaks his ankle!!
Panel 30: Teddy flailing arms, horrified facial expression, hopping around with a trap on his foot.
Panel 31: Teddy takes off the trap, looking very much in pain.
Panel 32: Teddy removes the sleetipede's two candy-cane antennae. He is preparing to use them not just to help him walk, but also to check for additional animal traps in the yard. His need for reassurance that nothing weird is going on is getting stronger, which explains why he is now resorting to trespassing (and stealing) to give himself reassurance that nothing supernatural is going on.
Panel 33: Teddy tiptoes around the yard, poking the ground randomly with the candy canes he took from the sleetipede.
Panel 34: Teddy begins using his new candy canes as he limps home.
Panel 35: A flashback of the Banner residence yard, exaggerated where everything seems more frightening than it really is (gargoyles and sleetipede appear nefarious and sentient). This scene can be a reflection of Teddy's paranoid mind.
Panel 36: Teddy continues his walk home. He is trying to hum to himself to distract himself from his paranoia.
Panel 37: Teddy is facing his home, standing outside. Warm light is coming out the windows, and the lights from the strung X-mas lights are shining brightly. Teddy's bedroom window can be seen. The Christmas lights surrounding his window are also shining.
Panel 38: Tattered "Home is where the Heart is" rug, disheveled and with lots of dirt and footprints, a sort of symbolism for "mundane home life." Like when passive people get called "doormats." A metaphor for Teddy being passive, meek, and timid. It's a contrast to the floor rug's message of optimism.
Panel 39: Teddy enters the kitchen, still using his candy canes. Karen appears confused and worried at the same time. Teddy looks flushed.
Panel 40: Teddy and Karen are sitting in the car at the ER. Teddy appears in pain, maybe sweaty.
Panel 41: Medical staff are clamoring around as they prepare to take Teddy into the Emergency Room. Teddy appears somewhat in pain. Karen smiles, slightly in jest and mocking Teddy's foolishness.
Panel 42: Teddy appears at the entrance of the waiting room, Karen looking up past her magazine. Teddy is wearing one of those medical boots and holding his Sorel boot in his hand.
Panel 43: Teddy and Karen are walking towards the exit of the waiting room.
Panel 44: A woman is being led into the ER with an ice pick jabbed all the way through her hand! There is a lot of blood. Teddy and Karen are staring at her.
Panel 45: Teddy and Karen standing outside the car, not getting inside yet. Dear Diary

Chapter 6: A Rather Slippery Slope...
Eve after Eve, December 25, 2015, 7:00 pm

Panel 1 (full page, start of chapter 6): Maybe something like killer roses coming after Teddy (with their stems in a vase full of evil water). This could also be a sort of nightmare sequence.
Panel 2: Teddy is sitting on his bed, staring at his TV, clicking the remote as he checks for channels.
Panel 3: The TV screen fills up most of the screen, partial footage of a dead man being hauled out of a wishing well. Pennies and coins fall off of him as he is being pulled out.
Panel 4: Teddy changes channel. It shows the picture of a man who slit his own throat in a courtroom after his guilty verdict was read. The image shows the man holding the razor to his throat, but the image is frozen/paused just before he actually kills himself. Panel 5: Teddy changes channel.
Panel 6: Teddy clicks off the TV.
Panel 7: Teddy sits at his desk in front of the computer.
Panel 8: There is a close-up shot of a list Teddy is making called "Benefits of Water."
Panel 9: There is a close-up shot of the back of the paper, a list entitled "Cons of Water."
Panel 10: Teddy drumming his pencil on his chin, deep in thought.
Panel 11: Teddy crumples up his list and tosses it at the window.
Panel 12: Teddy lying on his back, staring at the ceiling, hands behind his head. Ceiling fan buzzing.
Panel 13: a scary shot of a giant blob monster devouring anything it touches! This is a metaphor for the water affecting whatever it touches. The image is exaggerated to show Teddy's affinity for "catastrophizing" or assuming the worst.
Panel 14: Pic of Lydia Jales Obituary, Teddy's grandma and Derek's mother, around 75 years old. The pic is a recent one, showing her wearing informal attire.
Teddy's Science Journal, Water Experiment Setup
Teddy Science Journal: Results of Water Experiment

Issue 4
Chapter 7: Daydreams and/or Nightmares
January 25, 2016

Panel 1 (full page, start of chapter 7): A very creepy piggy bank inside a snowglobe (the snow is falling in the snowglobe, as if it was just shaken!!). The snowglobe is sitting on top of a dresser or nightstand. The pig has a sort of mischievous smirk, as if it is up to something nefarious.
Panel 2: Teddy is talking to Sylvia Koch (school counselor). Sylvia is a twenty-something school counselor. Her office is fairly standard, with a desk, a bookshelf, and pictures of plants on the walls. Teddy is on La-Z-Boy type chair, Sylvia is using her office chair. Sylvia is wearing a maxi skirt. Sylvia is writing in a notepad as she listens. Teddy is wearing a school uniform. There is a coffee table near Teddy, and it has a box of tissues in case Sylvia's clients need to cry. There is also a wicker basket holding fidgets (for anxiety) like fidget cubes or spinners.
Panel 3: An abstract and surreal pic of the front of the piggy bank. There are Rorschach ink blots surrounding the pig, and other various symbols of dreamland archetypes (dollar signs, z's, moons, stars, etc.). Have fun and be creative :)
Panel 4: Creepy expression of pig ("cold hard stare, sardonic smile"). The bank is very old, like something from an old Bugs Bunny cartoon. It has a wide-mouth grin. The panel shows a coin being dropped into the slot by Teddy's hand.
Panel 5: Teddy and Sylvia conversing. Teddy looks curious.
Panel 6: A Piggy bank is shown in a dreamscape, a sign above saying "Snowy Day Fund."
Panel 7: A view of little cars buzzing on the streets below (from the view of a 50-story building). This is a flashback from Teddy's dream.
Panel 8: Dream-Teddy dropping multiple coins into the creepy bank, as if the "pig" was insatiable and had an endless expanse of space and appetite to collect the coins.
Panel 9: Sylvia and Teddy talking in the office, creative angle. Sylvia is leaning forward, taking in the story, every word. She is also scribbling in her notepad.
Panel 10: Dream Teddy using his other hand, reaching into his other pocket, and dropping more coins.
Panel 11: Teddy's bedroom, but Dream Teddy is 80 years old!! Same clothes (school uniform). The bank is sitting on a scale. He is dreaming that he is in his own room! At this point, it feels very real to Teddy!
Panel 12: Dream Teddy holding the bank above his head, ready to smash it on the floor!!
Panel 13: Pig is slammed against the floor with force (but not breaking!!).
Panel 14: Dream Teddy tries again! Pig does not break!
Panel 15: Dream Teddy picks up the pig and stares at the creepy face. It looks menacing and is even revealing teeth!
Panel 16: Dream Teddy tries to smash it using a baseball bat. Does not break.
Panel 17: Dream teddy peering inside the coin slot of the bank.
Panel 18: A virtual landscape inside the bank that was much larger than the inside of the pig. There are well-sculpted "snow banks" littered around (actual bank vaults made from ice and snow). And the banks are guarded by snowcrows (snowmen dressed in shabby clothing, similar to scarecrows).
Panel 19: Sylvia and Teddy in the office. Teddy is using a fidget spinner.
Panel 20: Dream Teddy throws the bank right through his bedroom window.
Panel 21: Teddy looks at the ground below. People are scampering around, lining their pockets with coins (as the piggy bank broke on the ground below). The coin pile is much larger than what would normally fit into a real piggy bank.
Panel 22: Piggy bank is shattered on pavement, his face is oddly completely intact!
Panel 23: Dream Teddy pounding on elevator door with reckless abandon. It doesn't work!
Panel 24: Dream Teddy running down the stairs. You can see the number "25" on the door. Other tenants are clogging the stairwell. Each tenant was wearing normal clothing. But each had a number on their back corresponding to what floor they lived on. Similarly, each tenant was also wearing the same number of gold necklaces as their floor number. Of course, feel free to estimate (there is no need to sketch exactly how many necklaces each resident was wearing!) Feel free to make the folks from the upper floors appear wealthier than those below (except for Teddy, as he can retain his same outfit).
Panel 25: Dream Teddy dashing down the steps, getting closer to the bottom as evidenced by the number "3" on the door. Other tenants are clogging the stairwell (wearing their numbers and necklaces as before).
Panel 26: Outside shot. Throngs of people of similar height and build are scampering around collecting the money. As stated before, they each have numbers on their backs and corresponding gold necklaces. The residents from the lower floors made it to the money before anyone else.

Panel 27: Counseling room, Sylvia and Teddy both leaning in towards each other. Sylvia appears just as interested in listening as Teddy is in speaking. Teddy is using sweeping arm motions using lots of body language.

Panel 28: A shot of a homeless man in a back alley, with a zero on his back. He is slouched against a dumpster (he is NOT wearing a number or any necklaces).

Panel 29: A shot of a wealthy person drinking wine in her art-loft at a house party, with drinks and cheese trays. The wealthy person is wearing number 46 on her back and wearing 46 gold necklaces.

Panel 30: Dream Teddy is standing in front of the debris of the broken pig. There is not a single coin to be found!

Panel 31: Dream Teddy picks up the pig's intact face and inspects it. Its creepy grin is intact.

Panel 32: Dream Teddy puts the "inside" of the face part up to his ear, as if listening to the sea in a seashell.

Panel 33: Dream Teddy finds a solitary coin from under a piece of debris and holds it up.

Panel 34: Dream Teddy walking back upstairs, more slowly than before.

Panel 35: Dream Teddy's bedroom is intact, except no bed.

Panel 36: Dream Teddy putting piggy bank together on top of dresser or night stand.

Panel 37: Dream Teddy holding up the last coin in a dramatic pose, as if it were some powerful McGuffin. The piggy bank has returned to its original state (it no longer has the menacing grin with teeth showing).

Panel 38: Dream Teddy plunks the last coin into the bank.

Panel 39: Teddy and Sylvia in session.

Panel 40: The inside of the bank looks different than before. There is now a depressing winter landscape, a barren wasteland of sorts. Teddy's bed is sitting in the middle of an empty parking lot. Dream Teddy is in bed. Snow is falling gently on the bed and everywhere around. There are rows and rows of snowmen, all dressed identically in ragged "scarecrow" garb, all staring at the bed like sunflowers staring at the sun. They are snowcrows!!

Panel 41: Similar scenery as before. The snowcrows are chanting: "Sticks and stones may break your bones, but words will never hurt you." You can use "music notes" to represent the chant if you wish.

Panel 42: Teddy and Sylvia in session.

Panel 43: Counseling office, real Teddy and Sylvia in convo.

Panel 44: Flashback of Teddy in his real bedroom, waking from the scary dream. He is standing by the bed, sweating profusely. The light is on. There is a crack in the window.

Panel 45: Flashback Teddy tears the blanket off the bed, revealing a sweaty silhouette of his body on the mattress.

Panel 46: A close shot of a snowglobe, the snow is falling as if it had just been shaken!! The snowglobe shows a snowman inside, standing next to a Christmas tree.

Panel 47: A close shot from the snowglobe's point of view, there is falling snow, and you can see Teddy's eyes peering towards the "camera."

Panel 48: Counseling room, Teddy and Sylvia.

Panel 49: Sylvia closes her notepad.

Panel 50: Teddy close up, his face looking inquisitive.

Chapter 8: Back to School
January 25, 2016

Panel 1 (full page to introduce chapter 8): Frosty the Snowman (the actual one from the story) is half-melted and in the process of dying (like from the song). His face looks terrified as he anticipates his own death.

Panel 2: Science classroom. There are college-style desks and a large wooden table in front of the room. The bell is ringing, class is over. Students are scurrying out the door. Teddy is readying himself to leave. He is carrying "The Hidden Messages of Water" by Masaru Emoto in his hands. There are two jars sitting on the table (more rice experiments).

Panel 3: Most students left, a couple still in the process of leaving. Humis spots Teddy holding the Emoto book "The Hidden Messages of Water," and is pointing at it.

Panel 4: A copious assortment of papers is neatly arranged on the large oak table in the front of the room. Humis is in the process of laying them out separately from each other. The papers are arranged near the two jars (also on the table). The jar on stage left says "bad vibes" on it, and the jar on the right says "good vibes" on it.

Panel 5: Insurance papers, you can see the "Pygmalion Logo" at the top, a flying pig with a happy expression on its face. There is a quote: "They say healthcare will become available when pigs fly. Guess what. The pigs have flown!"

Panel 6: Teddy is reading through one of the papers.

Panel 7: A shot of Las Vegas, maybe a roulette wheel and some slot machines. People gambling.

Panel 8: Teddy is looking at the forms with a fastidious and careful eye.

Panel 9: Teddy is pointing at some fine print on the form.

Panel 10: Another Pygmalion brochure, depicting a happy smiling family enjoying their insurance plans.

Panel 11: Teddy sets the papers down, knocking over the jar with the "bad vibes" label, spilling the water on the insurance paperwork!!

Panel 12: Teddy is cranking the paper dispenser, and he doesn't notice Humis carrying the two jars of water outside.

Panel 13: Professor Humis enters and walks back towards Teddy. Teddy is laying out the forms to dry.

Panel 14: Teddy is rushing out the door, Humis behind him.

Panel 15: Teddy and Humis are standing outside by the snowman. You can see "rice hair" on the snowman's head.

Panel 16: Teddy and Humis walk back towards school.

Panel 17: Teddy slips while in eye-shot of the snowman! He loses any semblance of gravitas.

Panel 18: Teddy on the ground, Humis trying to maintain his composure and fight his urge to laugh. Teddy is rubbing his pain.

Panel 19: Humis and Teddy are inside the building near the nurse's office, there is a large garbage can near the door. Teddy is pulling out the book Frosty the Snowman from the can.

Panel 20: Teddy pages through the book. There is a missing page, the very page where Frosty dies! Teddy notices it, but does not tell Humis.

Panel 21: Teddy tosses the book in the garbage.

Panel 22: Shot of Anomaly Academy from the outside, sort of ominous.

Panel 23: Shot of book in garbage can, sort of creepy like. A drop of blood from Teddy's hand can be seen on the cover of the book (on the snowman). Teddy's Diary

----

Issue 5
Chapter 9: A Snowball's Chance in Hell...
February 8, 2016 (Monday)

Panel 1 (full page to introduce chapter 9): A close-up shot of a Pygmalion Insurance brochure. It shows a pig with Monarch butterfly wings (the pig bears a slight resemblance to the piggy bank's expression). The pig is flying over a still lake. There is a barefoot farm boy skipping rocks across the still waters. The "Pygmalion Insurance" logo is written in a somewhat gothic font. It's very creepy and ominous!

Panel 2: Classroom, all students turning around in their seats and looking at the back of the room (some agape) at Professor Humis limping towards the front of the classroom. He is on crutches and has a neck brace. His right arm is broken and in a cast. One of his legs is also broken.

Panel 3: Humis and Teddy can be seen in the panel.

Panel 4: Professor Humis is standing in front of the podium, a smiling countenance painted across his face and demeanor.

Panel 5: Teddy scribbles on a piece of paper.

Panel 6: Professor Humis is speaking. Students are listening intently.

Panel 7: Teddy is writing in a notebook again.

Panel 8: Justin Banner (goth dressage) standing up and pointing at Humis.

Panel 9: Jane raises her hand. The professor is pointing at her, indicating that she can speak.

Panel 10: Humis is describing what happened to him and what caused his accident. He is shown driving a car on a standard two-lane highway (head-on traffic approaching in the left lane), and it is raining/snowing/sleeting heavily on his windshield. His wipers are working fine. You can see lots of traffic around him.

Panel 11: First-person view of Humis, from inside the car. His wipers suddenly stopped, and you could not see out the window. Perhaps use some sort of visual mechanism to denote that the next few panels are a flashback of the accident.

Panel 12: Humis is shown skidding into oncoming traffic!!

Panel 13: Humis crosses lanes and smashes into an oncoming car, glass shattering, totaling both cars!

Panel 14: Humus on a stretcher. The female driver of the other car is standing next to ambulance workers. She is completely fine, except for rubbing her head after some whiplash.

Panel 15: Humis is standing in the classroom. He does a formal (exaggerated) bow.

Panel 16: Class is over, students getting up and milling about, bell ringing. Teddy is near Humis.

Panel 17: Teddy and Humis in convo.

Panel 18: Teddy walking home from school, head down, looking depressed and anxious. The snowman near where David died by the fire hydrant is visible.

Panel 19: Teddy reaches for his door-knob and notices a monarch butterfly on the door knob. Teddy's diary

Chapter 10: The Carrot and Stick Principle
February 12, 2016 (Friday)

Panel 1 (full page panel to kick off chapter 10): To go along with the chapter title, it's only fitting to show our friend Frosty with his carrot nose and sticks for arms. He also has coal for eyes and stones for his mouth and abdomen (to represent buttons). All 4 of these items on the snowman are also metaphors/symbolism for consequences for our behaviors: the carrot and stick principle (reward and punishment), "sticks and stones may break your bones," and receiving coal for Christmas (or the coal in hell for that matter). Fire hydrant is visible, perhaps spewing blood, like a nightmare referencing what happened to poor David. Also, the two stones that formerly formed the snowman's "grin" mysteriously fell out, giving him a blank and ominous expression instead of a smile. The snowman also has a scarf. You can make him look even scarier than usual, like a caricature of nefariousness.

Panel 2: Teddy is admiring the snowman, but also curious and somewhat anxious. Jane is hiding behind the snowman, ready to give Teddy a jumpscare. Again, the snowman is missing some of the stones from the edges of his smile that formerly made him grin.

Panel 3: Teddy spots the missing stones on the ground near the snowman.

Panel 4: Teddy places stones back in the snowman's mouth

Panel 5: Jane jumps out from behind the snowman! Teddy looks horrified, almost like a manga/anime chibi expression. Jane is recording the scenario with her phone! The fire hydrant is nearby also. Jane is wearing a different color Converse shoe on each foot.

Panel 6: Teddy smacks the carrot out of the snowman's face. Jane is laughing hysterically.

Panel 7: Teddy places the carrot back into the snowman's face. Jane is still filming.

Panel 8: Jane is watching the video she just recorded. She looks very amused.

Panel 9: Teddy is looking over Jane's shoulder as she is watching the video. There are a couple of people walking nearby.

Panel 10: A still frame of a video. There is a hazy figure that kind of looks like David standing some distance from the snowman. It also sort of looks like he is wearing his usual black leather jacket. It's not super clear, though. It could go either way.

Panel 11: Teddy and Jane in a somewhat tense convo. They are both looking at the still frame.

Panel 12: Jane and Teddy looking somewhat angrily at each other, as if a small argument. But it's also partly in good fun.

Panel 13: Teddy and Jane are smiling in a friendly, caring way.

Panel 14: Teddy and Jane continue their conversation.

Panel 15: Jane and Teddy both look worried, but for different reasons.

Panel 16: A sombre sight, students crying in hallways, some comforting each other. Teachers mingling. Sylvia Koch was walking briskly down the hall. Teddy and Jane look confused and curious.

Panel 17: Humis's desk, empty. There is a sort of ominous vibe about it. The classroom (real) skeleton is visible, adding to the ominous ambiance.

Panel 18: Teddy and Jane are sitting in adjacent desks, in conversation. You can see Humis's vacant desk.

Panel 19: The school counselor, Sylvia Koch, stands next to Teddy and Jane. She is wearing her usual maxi skirt.

Panel 20: Close shot of Sylvia, with an exaggerated "chirpy" smile, trying her best to soothe the woes of the world.

Panel 21: Sylvia kneels down to the eye level of Teddy and Jane. Teddy and Jane are tearing up, drops running down their faces.

Panel 22: Sylvia is not crying, but she looks crestfallen and sombre, an empathetic "counselor face" when people are experiencing loss.

Panel 23: Jane scowls at Teddy.

Panel 24: Scene of Professor Humis driving on the frozen lake in a different car (could use a pickup for this scene). You can see the ice is broken and the truck is half-submerged!!

Panel 25: Sylvia forces a small, caring smile. Jane and Teddy are tearing up and sobbing.

Panel 26: Sylvia pats Teddy's shoulder and starts to make her egress as she makes her rounds to other students.

Panel 27: Jane scowls at Teddy

Panel 28: Jane looks caring, being more empathetic to the pain Teddy is feeling. She takes his hand. Teddy's Diary

Issue 6

Chapter 11: Love is an Existential Illusion (and the march of the Blizzard Wizards)
Valentine's Day, February 14, 2016

Panel 1 (full page to kick off chapter 11): Snowcrows are scattered across the school playground. They look almost like scarecrows on a field. There are a few crows visible, keeping their distance from the snowcrows.
Panel 2: Jane and Teddy are inside a greenhouse attached to Jane's home. There is a corner sectioned off where Jane has been doing water experiments using carnivorous plants (Sundews, Venus Fly Traps, Cobra Lillies, and Pitcher Plants).
Panel 3: Closer view of the carnivorous flora.
Panel 4: Teddy and Jane are standing in front of the plants.
Panel 5: Teddy hands Jane two seed packets for her parents' greenhouse, one Spearmint and the other Peppermint. You can see the words on the close-up shots of the seed packets.
Panel 6: Teddy and Jane are looking at the plants with a curious gaze. Jane sets the seeds on the table.
Panel 7: Teddy and Jane gazing at plants.
Panel 8: Teddy's face blushes. Jane looks irritated, in a funny way.
Panel 9: All four varieties of plants (each variety split into three groups).
Panel 10: Wide shot of Teddy and Jane conversing in the Greenhouse.
Panel 11: Three groups of Venus Fly Traps (control, negatively watered, and positively watered). Teddy looks worried.
Panel 12: Close shot of Venus Fly Trap. The size of the Venus flytraps in the control group is average size. The size of the traps in the negatively watered lot is visibly more disheveled. Those in the positively watered lot are visibly the largest of all three groups.
Panel 13: A medical diagram of an ulcer.
Panel 14: Jane and Teddy are looking at each other. Jane looks curious, but Teddy looks worried.
Panel 15: Jane's face only, as if staring at Teddy.
Panel 16: Teddy begins watering some random plants/flowers in Jane's mother's greenhouse. Jane is walking with him.
Panel 17: Teddy sets down the water bucket, looking offended. Jane finds a stool to sit on.
Panel 18: Jane has an offended expression.
Panel 19: Teddy sits on the floor, near Jane's stool, brooding and looking glum.
Panel 20: Different angle, maybe even from above their heads, as they converse.
Panel 21: A shot of the school yard. Snowcrows are scattered around the school yard!
Panel 22: A scene showing fellow classmate Justin Banner holding one of his gargoyles towards the blizzard-infused sky. You can also see lightning, a very rare sight during a snowstorm!!
Panel 23: Kids are shown building legions of snowcrows with the "evil snow."
Panel 24: Jane is shown smashing a snowcrow with a shovel! The scene is drawn exaggerated, as Teddy pictures a heroine kicking ass. In some ways, Teddy doesn't even believe it actually happened and thinks Jane is making it up.
Panel 25: Jane is melting a snowcrow on the school barbecue grill!! As before, the scene is bigger than life, Jane sees roasting snowcrows like Crimson Reds in Resident Evil.
Panel 26: Jane gets off her stool and helps Teddy up from the floor.
Panel 27: Jane hugs Teddy, smiling and laughing a little bit.
Panel 28: Jane and Teddy are looking at each other.
Panel 29: Another shot of the original snowman "Frosty" (the one by the red fire hydrant).
Panel 30: "Frosty" wearing a top hat and holding a cane, dancing like a tap dancer, as if a sentient human.
Panel 31: Inside the greenhouse again, Teddy is looking at the Cobra Lilies. Jane is pointing towards the spade and sack of soil in the corner. There is a large 20-gallon pot near Jane. It's about 20 inches deep and 20 inches in circumference.
Panel 32: Teddy returns, spade in one hand, soil in the other. The spade is bent up, rusty, with burn marks, and very disheveled looking. Maybe some burn marks on the handle.
Panel 33: Jane is busy shoveling dirt into the large pot.
Panel 34: Jane hands Teddy a spade.
Panel 35: Jane is busy putting a small tree into the pot.
Panel 36: Image of Teddy's room. There are water bottles sitting on the floor. You can see burning incense and music notes denoting relaxation music being played in their presence.
Panel 37: A fun shot of a vampire recoiling from garlic.
Panel 38: A portrait of Lydia Jales, Teddy's grandma. She is smiling and looks like a nice person.
Panel 39: Jane gives Teddy one of her mother's cacti as Teddy leaves.
Panel 40: Shot of cactus, it's in good health.
Panel 41: Jane holds open a sack as Teddy carefully puts the cactus in.
Panel 42: Shot from inside the greenhouse, but looking out the open door. There is rain, snow, and sleet coming down hard.
Panel 43: Teddy is standing outside the door, staring at the heavens, holding up his palms to catch the rain and snowflakes. His sack is hanging from his wrist.
Teddy's Diary

Chapter 12: Not responsible for accidents
March 3, 2016

Panel 1 (full page panel to kick off chapter 12): A yellow pylon says "not responsible for accidents" near the original snowcrow by the fire hydrant. There is an eeriness here, maybe showing a blood trail coming out of the yellow pylon. Maybe show a kid on crutches, another in a wheelchair, etc.
Panel 2: Seventh and eighth grade students having fun in the tennis court, being a bit rowdy and roughshod. Teddy is sitting on the swing watching, wearing his canteen. Jane is next to him.
Panel 3: A boy is writhing in pain on the floor of the tennis court, as he twists his ankle. Teddy is pointing towards the scene.
Panel 4: A montage of images, depicting various school yard injuries (broken arms/legs, head injuries, cuts/scrapes, etc.).
Panel 5: Teddy is taking notes (inconspicuously) in his notebook.
Panel 6: Students are quitting badminton on the tennis court and are readying a gym rope for tug of war. There is an audience of snowcrows around the outside of the tennis court, staring towards it.
Panel 7: Large sixth grader James Worth is on the tennis court, prepping to play tug of war. He is a Tug-of-War champion. His nickname is "Tugboat."
Panel 8: More visual of the rope being readied for battle. The floor of the court is laced with a hard-packed icy layer of snow, made tight from the

tromping of boots over days. There are four sixth graders on one side, including James Worth (3 males and 1 female), and five fifth graders on the other side (3 males and 2 females) to offset any unfair advantage the older students might hold.

Panel 9: Spectators are gathered to watch the upcoming battle. The recess monitor (who usually spends her time at the elementary playground side) is there near the tennis court, holding a "Not Responsible for Accidents" pylon!

Panel 10: Contestants are pulling for dear life! They are pretty much at a standstill. Mary Thompson is looking scared.

Panel 11: Tug of war action. The older students are winning in this panel, they are pulling the other side closer to them! Students are grunting and groaning.

Panel 12: Justin and his mates are tying the rope around their bare hands.

Panel 13: The older students are gaining traction!

Panel 14: The younger students find more traction, and the tide again starts to turn. Both sides are sweating and tired.

Panel 15: The tug of war rope jettisons away from the older students like a rubber band, taking the fingers of the older students with it (including Tugboat/James Worth).

Panel 16: Students are screaming, bloody fingers on the ground. Mary, Jane, and Teddy make a mad dash towards the scene inside the icy tennis court (Mary leaves her pylon near Frosty the Snowcrow, near the fire hydrant where David died).

Panel 17: More blood and gore. Freaky depictions. Kids in pain (including Tugboat).

Panel 18: More shots of "scene of the crime." Students are screaming, fingers missing. Mary is looking frantic. Jane, Teddy, and Mary are inside the court. Jane already has her phone out, dialing 911.

Panel 19: Recess monitor Mary can be seen picking up a coffee can just outside the entrance of the tennis court (it's the makeshift ashtray she always used when smoking outside). You can see cigarette butts at the bottom.

Panel 20: Mary is holding a coffee can towards Jane, onlookers present, etc. Mary is in a bit of a mad panic, not knowing where to start.

Panel 21: The original snowcrow can be seen, with a more sinister expression. The two stones on each side of the mouth that formed his smile have since fallen out. The "Not responsible for Accidents" pylon can also be seen near the snowcrow. Jane is holding the coffee can, Teddy next to her, looking for fingers.

Panel 22: Jane and Teddy are finger hunting. Jane is holding the can. Teddy is holding a finger (with a ring still on it) over Jane's can ready to drop it.

Panel 23: Jane hands can to Mary. Teddy is nearby. An ambulance can be seen approaching. Mary looks worried.

Panel 24: Teddy and Jane are on their swings, not moving. Teddy's Diary

BLAKE ALB

Blake Alb (Snowcrow, The Fairgrounds) is a writer with a passion for stories that stray from the beaten path. He has an MS in psychology and has worked extensively in the field of mental health. He attributes his psychology degree as playing a significant role in providing a wellspring of ideas for storytelling. He is a big fan of all things geeky, with a penchant for Japanese anime/manga, fantasy, science fiction, and video games. He also enjoys British comedy and performing improv. He has published a variety of short stories and novels.

JOHN DAVIES

John Davies has worked in the comics and entertainment industry as a multimedia illustrator for the better part of 34 years. His love of drawing came about when he was 5 years old. Growing up in Southern California gave him a great opportunity to flourish with creative contacts. His studies grew and centered around fine arts (which he also has a degree). Utilizing these skills, John began working as an illustration designer, penciler, and inker (including positions on set at Warner Bro. Studios). John has worked on several published periodicals within the comic book industry for many independent companies. He has also held a position within a studio environment that produced illustrations for DC Comics. John is also working on Station 39 for Charter Comics, along with multiple cover projects for independent publishers, music groups, etc.

LIEH PENA

Brazilian native Lieh Pena has been drawing as a hobby since childhood and professionally since 2009 when he illustrated his first book, "Zamba's Journey" ("A Jornada de Zamba" in Portuguese). He also illustrated "The Little Cowboy" parts 1 and 2 — a Northeast Brazilian parody of "The Little Prince". His illustrating works also include covers for other books, academic text papers, and a health booklet. In the field of comic books, his works include a few independent productions (yet to be published) and a political comic, plus his own comic project (yet to be finished). He also has a degree in English Language Teaching & Literature from the Universidade de Pernambuco (UPE). However, his love was always Sequential Arts in any form (cartoon, manga, graphic, etc.). For that reason, as a self-taught artist, he always tried to develop abilities related to such media, like penciling, inking, digital coloring, and lettering.